THE HALL OF A THOUSAND DOORS

THE HALL OF A THOUSAND DOORS

By

Christopher David Sturdevant

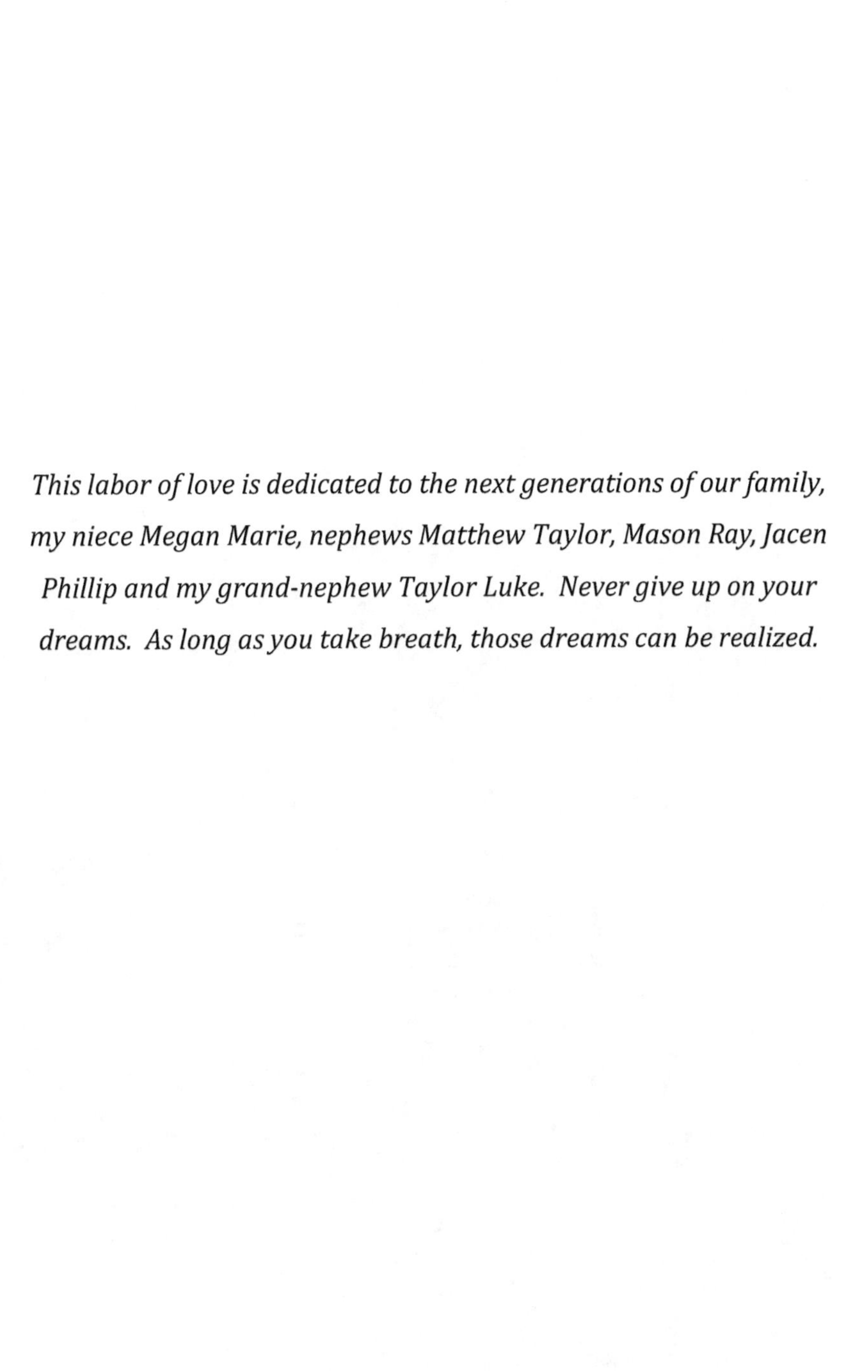

This labor of love is dedicated to the next generations of our family, my niece Megan Marie, nephews Matthew Taylor, Mason Ray, Jacen Phillip and my grand-nephew Taylor Luke. Never give up on your dreams. As long as you take breath, those dreams can be realized.

Acknowledgements

There are so many people in my life to acknowledge and thank for their contribution in helping this book to become a reality.

First and foremost, to my father and mother for their constant love and support throughout the years. If not for the lessons of life they taught me along the way, I would not be the person I am today. To Mom, for being my first reader, several times over, for acting as a sounding board for my ideas, and for helping me to realize that I have a story worth sharing with the world.

To my older brother, Robert, and his exceptional talents in photography. His skillful eye captured the perfect images used on my biography page and on the back cover of this novel. To my younger sister, Jennifer, for her help with the marketing of this book and to my younger brother Daniel, for his support to continue this process until its completion.

I also want to say a special thank you to Robert G. Scruggs III, my high school sophomore English teacher and mentor. It was he, who long ago, helped me to discover my talent and love for writing. He was there at the beginning to read over my initial works, offer constructive advice and help me to hone my skills as a writer. Now, 33 years later, he has offered his vast amount of knowledge and experience to serve as the literary editor for this book.

I want to acknowledge and thank Rebecca Koehnen for taking on the task of creating the artwork for this book. Her extraordinary skills as an artist and illustrator come shining through on the cover art and illustrations within this book.

To my entire circle of family and friends, for their love and encouragement all along the way.

Finally, to Ron Lammert, Colin Hart and the knowledgeable staff at HPN Books, 11535 Galm Road, Suite 101, San Antonio, TX, 78254, for making the self-publishing of this book an easier and painless process to understand.

Introduction

These days, Hollywood is having great successes with the retelling of the traditional fairy tales in both theaters and on television. *Snow White and the Huntsman, Hansel and Gretel*, and *Jack the Giant Slayer* are all recent live-action box office hits that take the stories of old and give them new life.

Likewise, ABC's *Once Upon A Time* and NBC's *Grimm*, take the essence of the classics and puts a new spin on them. Seeing how well audiences have reacted to these retellings, I felt that the time was right for the story of *The Hall of a Thousand Doors* to be told.

The *Hall of a Thousand Doors* has been a work in progress for almost three decades now. After all of these years, the adventurous journey of my child hero, Alex DaSilva, is finally ready to get underway.

The beginnings of this story go back to the year 1985. Its concepts originated from a poem I had written a couple of years before. This poem featured a young man who found himself trapped in a hallway. Behind each door that lined the hallway were scenes from his life.

When I began to entertain ideas of turning this poem into a short story, I replaced the young man with a child, and each of the doors became a portal leading to one of the many fairy tales he has heard about, all of his life. Alex's rival in this tale is the dark wizard Nagama, who uses his magical powers to create chaos and change the happy endings of these stories. With guidance from a beautiful sorceress, Alex soon realizes he has both the power and the knowledge to set things right. Knowing that a showdown with the powerful wizard is inevitable, he vows to stop the villain, once and for all.

This children's adventure novel revisits the worlds of some of our most treasured fairy tales in a way never before imagined. The tales in which Alex visits in this book are the time honored classics given to us by Jacob and Wilhelm Grimm, better known throughout the literary world as the Brothers Grimm.

As a first time self-published author, I am excited to bring this story to the world, but I need your help and support to spread the word about this book. It is a story that can be enjoyed by people of all ages. For more information about the author, how to order a copy of this book, and to read about other books in progress, please feel free to visit my website at *www.ajourneywithwords.com*. You can also follow my progress on Facebook by liking my author page at *www.facebook.com/ajourneywithwords/*.

I hope that my readers get as much pleasure out of reading this story as I had writing it. Now, turn the page and let the journey begin.

PROLOGUE

Prologue

The classroom was in a state of utter chaos. The students' rebellious behavior was so bad that it was close to becoming a full blown riot. The teacher, Miss Tahlaria, was at her wit's end. She stood next to the chalkboard at the front of the classroom and tried several times to calm the kids down, but failed to bring the class back to some semblance of order.

Alexander "Alex" DaSilva was in the back left corner of the room watching the rowdy drama unfold. He sat there at his desk in disbelief, as he tried to comprehend just what was going on.

He watched his teacher's vain attempts to calm the class down. His fellow classmates were acting out in many ways. Many of them were yelling and screaming. Some ran around the room, weaving in and out between the tables and chairs, while others were banging their hands, drumming on their desks. A few of them were even throwing things across the room, like wads of paper and crayons. The bigger kids were picking on the smaller ones. It was absolute pandemonium.

One particular kid, Billy Smith, a known bully around the school, noticed that Alex was not joining in on the craziness and started to give him a hard time. Alex tried his best to ignore the boy as Billy started to tease him. "Ah, look everyone, the teacher's pet is sitting in his chair and being a good little boy."

Billy then wadded up a piece of paper and threw it at Alex, hitting him in the shoulder.

Alex's first instinct was to glare angrily at Billy.

"What? You gonna do something about it?" taunted Billy as he tried to get a rise out of Alex.

Alex did not respond to Billy. He just turned his head away and went back to ignoring the bully.

"That's what I thought, you little chicken."

Miss Tahlaria's started to raise her voice, getting louder and louder, until she was practically yelling across the room. She was trying her best to be heard over the deafening roar of the children gone wild. Every effort she tried seemed ineffective at bringing the class back under some measure of control.

Frustrated and a little angry, she finally threw her hands up in the air, sighed, and left the room to get help. Alex got up from his desk, followed her out of the classroom and into the hallway. There, he saw a number of teachers gathering. He could hear the students in the other classrooms throughout the school acting the same way as the kids in his class. For some unknown reason, the students were not listening to their teachers.

"What has gotten into them?" asked Miss Tahlaria.

"I have no clue," answered another teacher. "It's like they all went crazy all of a sudden. One of my students actually threw a chalkboard eraser at me."

Just then, the school's principal, Mr. Thompson, came around the corner. He was walking down the hallway at a fast pace in the direction of the gathering of teachers. The teachers met up with him and reported the unusual behavior of their students. Mr. Thompson was not in the least bit surprised by what they had to say, and he informed them that the same thing was happening all over the school.

"We must regain control over the classrooms," he concluded, "now, before something happens, and one of the kids gets seriously hurt."

"How do you propose we accomplish that?" asked one of the other teachers.

The principal looked at each one of the teachers before him and then replied, "We will have to do this one classroom at a time. We will send a group of teachers into the first classroom and together, they will work to calm the children down. When that class is under control, we will leave one of the teachers behind and move on to the next class, and the next, and so forth." He pointed towards the school security guard, and the PE coaches and said, "The five of you will act as my hall monitors. Your job is to cover the hallways and exits to ensure that none of the children leave the school property."

The principal suddenly stopped and looked just beyond the gathering of teachers. He noticed Alex standing there in the hallway. The look on the principal's face was tense. "Alex, why are you not in your classroom?" he barked out.

Before Alex could say anything, Miss Tahlaria spoke up for him. "Alex is the only kid in my class who was not acting out. He must have followed me into the hallway, when I left the classroom to get help."

Mr. Thompson looked back to Alex. His facial expression relaxed a bit, and then he calmly said, "Thank you, Alex, for not getting caught up in all of this. Why don't you go to the library and wait there while the teachers, and I try to calm everyone down? I will come get you when things get back to normal."

"Yes sir," said Alex, as he nodded.

"Good boy."

Alex did as he was instructed and went down the hallway, straight to the library. There, he told the librarian about the madness that was going on, and that he was asked, by Mr. Thompson, to come here to the library and wait until the situation was back under control. The librarian offered to help Alex find a book to read while he waited, to pass the time. Together, they walked over to the bookshelves and after a few minutes of browsing, he settled on the book *Pinocchio.* Most kids his age were into the stories of *Harry Potter* or *Percy Jackson*, but Alex was different. He had a love for the classics.

He took the book and went to the corner of the library. There, he sat down in one of the bean bag chairs and began to read aloud, trying to drown out the turmoil happening throughout the school. Since there were no other children in the room, the librarian did not mind Alex breaking the golden rule of "No talking in the library." She smiled at him.

"*Pinocchio*, by Carlo Collodi. *Geppetto, a poor old wood carver, was making a puppet from a tree branch. 'You shall be my little boy,' he said to the puppet, 'and I shall call you Pinocchio.'*"

Alex read on.

The librarian returned to her desk. There, she sat and listened as the young boy read the story. She knew that reading was a great love of his.

As time went by, Alex noticed the hallways were getting quieter and quieter. Finally, the sounds of children yelling and screaming had stopped. It took almost two hours for the school faculty to go from class to class and regain control over the thirty classrooms in the school.

Mr. Thompson finally came to the door of the library. He looked around for a moment, searching for Alex. The librarian pointed across the room. He turned in the direction to which she had pointed and found Alex sitting on the bean bag chair, still reading the library book aloud. He walked over to Alex and in a hushed tone, called out to him.

"Alex?"

Alex stopped his reading of *Pinocchio* and looked up. "Yes, sir?"

"You can go back to your class now, son. We have the situation under control. Thank you again for not being a part of the problem."

"Yes sir, and you are welcome. Any clue as to why the rest of the kids were acting like that?"

"No, Alex, I still do not understand what started it all." He paused a moment to reflect and then said, "Miss Tahlaria is expecting you, so let's not keep her waiting."

"Yes sir."

Alex closed the book and got up from the bean bag chair. He returned the book to the librarian, then he walked out of the room, down the hallway and back into his classroom.

Mr. Thompson watched as Alex walked through the doorway, smiled, then returned to his office. He now had a mountain of paperwork to contend with as a result of the unusual behavior of his students, and he knew it was only a matter of time before parents would start calling once they learned of the day's events.

The rest of the day was fairly routine, almost like nothing ever happened. The kids were all back to normal, and yet this somehow troubled Alex.

When the bell sounded at 3PM, ending the school day, Alex tidied up his desk and packed up his backpack. He left the classroom and walked down the hall towards the door leading outside. He went around to front of the school, where the bus would pick him up, and take him home.

The bus ride home was relatively uneventful. There was no indication from the other kids that the turmoil at school ever happened. The kids were laughing and playing as the bus drove on.

When the bus finally dropped him off at his bus stop, his babysitter, Tricia, was there waiting for him. Tricia was a seventeen-year-old high school student who had been Alex's babysitter for almost three years now. She was red-headed and petite, and she was an extremely bright and responsible teenager. Her intuition and experience as a caregiver, told her right away that something was bothering Alex.

"Hey, Little Man. What's wrong?" she asked.

"Nothing."

"Are you sure?"

"Yeah," he said rather unconvincingly.

They walked around the block to where Alex lived. It was an older, white, two-story, four-bedroom, house with green trim. The lawn showed diligent and immaculate care.

Tricia walked up to the front door and unlocked it. They both went inside. Alex went straight upstairs to his room, where he dropped off his backpack. After stopping off to feed his fish, he came back downstairs to the living room and sat down in the easy chair.

Alex sat before the large bay window of his living room for an hour, gazing out at the world beyond. Tricia decided to let him be, for now. He was deep in thought over the events that had occurred earlier in his day at school. He was still trying to make sense of what caused the other kids to act the way they did. He was so preoccupied with those thoughts, that he did not even notice the door opening, or his mother, Sarah Anne DaSilva, coming home from work. She saw Alex sitting there, appearing a million miles away from the moment.

"Hi Sweetheart, how was your day?" she inquired.

Alex did not respond to her question, still appearing far off within his own thoughts.

"Alex?" she called out. When he did not respond again, Sarah walked across the room, over to where her son sat, and gently touched him on the shoulder. Startled by her touch, he jumped, bringing him back to the reality of the moment.

"I am so sorry, Honey. I didn't mean to scare you. Is everything alright?" she asked.

"Oh hi, Mom. How was your day?" he replied, in a somewhat flat tone.

"My day was busy as usual," she answered. "Lots of paperwork to go through, and it seemed like the phone never stopped ringing. But, I was asking you how your day went, and if everything was ok."

Alex hesitated before answering, searching for the right words to reply. Not finding them, he finally said, "It was...," he paused a moment. "Okay."

Sarah looked at her blond, blue-eyed son with doubt. Those blue eyes looked back at her, troubled, which was not normal for him. He was always so happy and upbeat. Smarter than most children his age, he had a strong sense of self, and he would make a fine leader someday if that was what he chose to do with his life. Finally, she said, "I am not too convinced about that. You seem rather distracted."

Alex turned in his chair to face his mom. He considered her to be the strongest, most beautiful woman, on Earth, as most nine-year-old sons do feel. She had long, curly blonde hair that bounced with every turn of her head. She had a smile that could light up the darkest and gloomiest of places. Like him, she had big blue eyes, and once again those eyes sparkled.

It had been just over two years since Alex's father had passed away. He was sick for a long time. Since then, it had been just the two of them. He knew that his mother had been depressed and lonely, but now, he could start to see signs that she was beginning to feel happy once again.

Alex sat, collecting his thoughts. Just then, Tricia, walked into the living room from the kitchen. She had been there working on her homework, awaiting Sarah's return from work.

"Oh, hi Mrs. DaSilva. How are you?" she asked.

"Hello, Tricia. I am doing great. How are you today?" replied Sarah.

"I am fine. By the way, I took the clothes out of the washer, dried them and then hung them on hangers for you," said Tricia.

"Thank you, Tricia. You did not have to do that, but it is very much appreciated."

"Well, I just like to help out wherever I can. Besides, it gives you more time to spend with Alex."

Sarah smiled at Tricia. She had come to work for Sarah back when her late husband got sick. Between his doctor's appointments and taking care of him at home, she needed the help. Though Tricia was still in her teens, she had always shown herself to be a very responsible young lady. That, and the fact that Alex adored her made the decision to hire her a no brainer.

Tricia continued, "I should be getting home, now. My mom will have dinner ready, soon." She went back into the kitchen, gathered up her things, and prepared to leave. As she walked towards the front door, she turned back to Sarah and said, "Oh, and about watching Alex this Saturday. I checked my schedule, and I don't have anything planned. So I will be able to come over and hangout with Little Man while you go in to work."

"Tricia, as always, you are a lifesaver. I don't know what I would do without you," said Sarah gratefully.

"I don't mind. Alex is a great kid, and you are always very generous with what you pay me," replied Tricia.

Sarah smiled again, "I pay you well because you take very good care of Alex, and you always help out even though you don't have to."

Sarah walked Tricia to the door and thanked her again for her thoughtfulness. When they were out of earshot from Alex, Tricia quietly said to Sarah, "Alex seems like he has something heavy, weighing on his mind. I tried to talk to him about it, but he played it off like nothing was wrong. He has been sitting there in that chair, looking out the window, since he got home from school."

"I noticed it when I walked in the door. I will have a talk with him about it," replied Sarah. "Thank you for letting me know."

Tricia turned back towards Alex and said, "I'll see you tomorrow, Little Man."

"Okay, Tricia. See you later," he replied.

Tricia smiled, then she turned to leave for her house across the street. Sarah waited until she had crossed the street and was safely inside her own house before closing the front door and returning to Alex. She sat down on the couch facing him.

"Okay. So why don't you tell me what's on your mind," she said.

Alex sighed, then he began to tell his mother about what happened at school that day.

"I think most, if not all the kids in my school, are going crazy."

Sarah laughed and asked, "Crazy? What makes you say that, Honey?"

Alex replied, "Well, it seemed like all the kids were getting into trouble for one thing or another. Nobody would listen to what any of the teachers were telling them to do, and it wasn't just in my class either. All of the classes in the school were having problems."

Sarah's expression took on a playful, stern look, "Wow! That sounds rather serious. I hope that does not include you."

Alex shook his head and with a look of pure innocence said, "No. I would never. I felt like I was the only one who was listening to the teacher. One of the other kids in my class started calling me 'Teacher's Pet' and giving me grief."

Sarah smiled at Alex as she ruffled his hair. "Well, don't let the other kids get to you. You did the right thing by listening to your teacher and staying out of trouble. I am so proud of you for not letting them pressure you into acting out. Why don't I make us some dinner, and we can talk about it some more?"

Alex smiled and nodded his head.

Sarah asked, "Is there anything in particular that you would like for supper?"

"Well," he pretended to think real hard, then said, "I could go for a grilled cheese sandwich, and some tomato soup."

Sarah stood up from the couch, bent over to kiss her son on the forehead and said, "Why am I not surprised that you want a grilled cheese sandwich and tomato soup?"

"It's comfort food, Mom," replied Alex, with a wink and a grin.

Sarah laughed and said, "You got it, Sweetheart." She then turned, walked into the kitchen and began making dinner.

Alex went back to looking out of the large bay window, his thoughts once again preoccupied with what happened earlier at school.

A few minutes later, Sarah called out to Alex from the kitchen, "Honey, can you come and set the table for me, please?"

"Sure thing, Mom."

Alex got up from the chair and walked into the kitchen. He went to the corner near the pantry to get a step stool and placed it below the cupboard, where the dishes were kept. Stepping up, he opened the cupboard door and pulled down the dishes, setting them on the counter. He opened the counter drawer and took out a couple of spoons and carried them and the dishes to the table and set them in their places.

Sarah stood at the stove, flipping the grilled cheese sandwiches. She smiled at her Little Man. When the sandwiches were finished, she placed them on a plate and carried the food to the table. She put the food down and grabbed the bowls, filling each of them with hot tomato soup. Finally, she went to the refrigerator and grabbed the gallon jug of milk. She poured two glasses and set them on the table. In the meantime, Alex waited for his mother to sit down before he took his seat. They both bowed their heads, and Sarah said a prayer over their meal.

Sarah began eating, but after several minutes, she noticed that Alex had barely touched his food.

"Not hungry, Sweetie?" she asked.

Alex was a bit distracted in his response. "What? Oh, sorry. I was still thinking about what happened at school. I don't understand why they were acting the way they did. Even the kids who never get into trouble were causing problems."

Sarah thought for a long moment and then said, "Maybe there will be a full moon outside tonight."

"No. I already thought about that," he smiled jokingly. "We only have a half-moon tonight."

They both laughed at Alex's joke and then Sarah said, "I know you are troubled by this, but I wish you would try to eat something. There is no reason to make yourself sick over this. Only you can be responsible for your own actions, and the other kids have to be responsible for theirs. It's a good thing that this bothers you though; it shows that you've got a good heart."

Alex smiled at his mother, then picked up his sandwich and began eating. When he was finished, he picked up his dishes and carried them to the sink. He turned and left the kitchen. Sarah called out to him.

"Thank you for taking your dishes to the sink."

"You're welcome," he called back.

"How about you get your homework out of the way, and then I will read to you before bed?"

Alex popped his head back into the kitchen. "Can you read *Beauty and the Beast* this time?" he asked excitedly.

"Again?" she sighed. "How many times have I read that one to you?"

"But Mom, I like that one."

Sarah laughed, "You like all of them. You just never seem to get tired of hearing those stories over, and over, and over again."

Alex pretended to pout.

Sarah raised her arms in surrender and said, "Alright. *Beauty and the Beast* it is."

Alex, in turn, raised his arms in victory and let out an excited, "Yes!" He turned around and quickly went up the stairs to his room. He picked up his book bag and pulled out his homework. Then, he sat down at his desk, and began working on his assignments.

While Alex worked on his homework, Sarah finished clearing the table. She rinsed the dishes and put them into the dishwasher. Once the dishes were loaded in the dishwasher, she filled the soap dispenser, closed the door and pushed the start button to begin the cleaning cycle. When the dishes were finished, she walked to the laundry room and grabbed the clothes that Tricia had hung up for her. She carried them up the stairs and put her clothes in her closet, then carried Alex's to his room and hung them in his closet.

Alex was still sitting at his desk, working on his math homework. Sarah looked over his shoulder to check on his progress.

"How's it coming?" she asked.

"I am working out the last couple of problems now, then I am done."

"Good work, Sweetie," she said as she bent down to kiss him on his forehead. "When you are finished, you can get ready for bed, and then we can start story time."

Sarah left the room to allow Alex time to finish up his homework. Rarely did she have to check his work. He always did quite well with his studies, but if there was ever something he did not understand, he always asked for her help.

Alex finished his homework and gathered up his books, placing them back into his book bag. He then went to the bathroom where he bathed, brushed his teeth and changed into his pajamas.

When he was finished getting ready for bed, he walked back to his room and went to the bookshelf filled with numerous hardbound books, and he took out *Beauty and the Beast* from the second shelf.

Sarah walked back into the room and asked, "Ready?"

Alex nodded his head, "Yes Ma'am."

"Okay, then, hop into bed."

Alex got into his bed and under the covers. Sarah laid down beside him. She opened the book and began reading.

"*Beauty and the Beast by Gabrielle-Suzanne Barbot de Villeneuve. Once upon a time, in a very far-off country, there lived a merchant who had been so fortunate in all his undertakings that he was enormously rich. As he had, however, six sons and six daughters, he found that his money was not too much to let them all have everything they fancied, as they were accustomed to.*"

Sarah continued reading to Alex, doing her best to imitate the voices of the characters as they spoke. This was their favorite thing in the world to do together. Every night, before bedtime, Sarah always read to him. This time was their time and nobody could take that away from them. No matter how busy life got or how crazy the world was, Alex could always count on a bedtime story. This tradition was started when Alex was only nine months old. Then, Sarah and her late husband, Alex Sr., would take turns reading Mother Goose rhymes and other fairy tales to him. Years later, when his father passed, Sarah vowed to keep the tradition alive.

After thirty minutes of reading, Sarah came near the end of the story.

"And then Beast asked Beauty one last time. 'Will you marry me?' Beauty replied, 'No Beast. I cannot, for I do not love you.' Beauty turns away from Beast and leaves him to go home. The sight of Beauty, leaving, saddens Beast. Days later, Beauty heard that Beast died of a broken heart. The End."

Alex turned to Sarah and looked strangely at her.

"What's wrong?" she asked.

"Mom. Read it right," he said.

"What are you talking about? I read it word for word."

"That's not how it's supposed to go. There's no happy ending," he challenged.

"Well, not every story has a happy ending, Sweetheart."

Alex looked carefully at the words in the book, and what he saw there, was exactly the way that Sarah had read the story. He was puzzled by this.

"Something is wrong," he said. "This is not the same story you've read to me before. Beauty is supposed to marry Beast and then they live happily ever after."

"This is the same book I always read," she countered. "See? Here is the note from your Dad."

Sarah turned the book back to the beginning and showed Alex the inside cover where there was an inscription written to him by his late father. The inscription read, *"To my son, Alex. Always remember that you should never judge a book by its cover, nor should you ever judge a person by the way they look on the outside. It's what is on the inside that counts. Love, Dad."* Alex indeed saw the words written to him from his father and he could not explain why he remembered this story ending so differently.

Finally, Sarah said, "I think you are getting your stories mixed up," as she set the book aside. "Okay. It's time for you to say your prayers and get some sleep."

Alex let go of the perplexing thoughts for the moment. He placed his hands together and began praying. "Now I lay me down to sleep. I pray the Lord my soul to keep. If I should die before I wake, I pray the Lord my soul to take. God bless Mama, Grandma and Grandpa, Oma and Opa, Aunt Kathy and Uncle Steve and Tricia. God bless Daddy in heaven. God bless all my friends and their families and God bless the poor people. Amen."

Sarah smiled at her son's simple, but powerful prayer.

She got up from the bed and returned the book to its place on the bookshelf. Then she walked back to the side of the bed, bent down and kissed Alex on the forehead. She tucked him in and walked out of the room, turning off the light as she left.

"I love you, Sweetheart. Good night. Sleep tight."

"Good Night, Mom. Love you, too."

Alex lay there in the dark, still troubled by the ending of *Beauty and the Beast*. He could not explain why he knew it should have ended differently. His thoughts churned away at the possibilities as he tried to understand how this could happen. Finally, his mind grew deeply tired from the day's events, and minutes later, he fell off into a sound sleep.

The night hours slowly passed by on the clock at his bedside. The room was strangely and eerily quiet. Alex was restless, tossing and turning, while he slept. His closed eyes moved rapidly, revealing that he was in the midst of dreaming.

Suddenly, there was the loud slam of a door that woke him, and he sat straight up.

PART I

Part I

When Alex first opened his eyes, he found himself to be in unfamiliar surroundings. From his vantage point, he could see that he was on the floor of a long, and what seemed like endless hallway. Flaming torches flickered above him, dimly lighting the hall in both directions. The floor beneath him was made of a smooth stone of some kind, and there were large wooden doors on either side of the hallway for as far as his eyes could see. Each door looked identical to the one next to it.

Alex crawled over to the door nearest him, and he raised himself up onto his knees. He examined the door more closely. It was made of a rough, dark-colored wood, probably mahogany or walnut. It was difficult to say for sure which in the low lighting of the torch-lit hallway. It had an ornate, golden trim with various types of jewels laid into it. The doorknob looked as if it were made of some sort of crystal, maybe even a large diamond.

Alex looked in one direction and then the other. There was nobody around but him. The only sound he could hear was the crackling of the fire from the torches on the walls above him.

"Mom?" he called out. "Are you there?"

But, there was no reply.

He stood up and began to walk down the long hallway, searching for his mother, Sarah.

"Mom!" he yelled more anxiously than the first time. "Where are you?"

Still nobody answered.

Again, he looked in both directions. He could not see a beginning nor an end to the hallway. He continued to walk down the seemingly endless hallway. With each step forward, Alex began to feel panic creeping into his thoughts. He could feel his pulse racing faster and faster, and his breathing had quickened, as well. He stopped and tried to ease his mind.

"Okay. Calm down, Alex. Take a deep breath and relax. So far there is nothing to be afraid of, just a long hallway with a bunch of harmless doors. Nothing to be afraid of..." he paused a moment, then said, "Yet..."

He began to walk forward once again.

After several minutes of exploring the hallway, Alex suddenly stopped and said, "Wait a minute. Maybe Mom is on the other side of one of these doors. I'll just open one up and see where it leads."

Alex stood there for a moment, debating on which door to choose. He strolled back and forth, from one door to the next, trying to decide. Then, a strange feeling suddenly came over him, and it drew him towards one of the doors. He walked to the massive doorway and reached out for the crystal-like doorknob. He turned the knob and pulled the door open.

Alex could not see anything beyond the threshold of the opened door, not even shadows. He looked up at the flaming torch on the wall next to the door. It was too high for him to reach. He squinted his eyes, trying to see if he could make anything out of the darkness before him, but he only saw blackness beyond the frame of the door. He hesitated a moment. Then, he drew in a deep breath, took a step forward and walked through the door.

There was a brilliant flash of blinding light, and the only thing Alex saw for several moments, were stars. He rubbed his eyes and turned back around in the direction from which he had come. The doorway that should have been there behind him had vanished. His eyes darted around in all directions, searching for the door he had just come through. He thought maybe it was possible he had become disoriented after coming through it, but everywhere he looked, he saw no sign of the door. It was gone. He was at a loss to explain how this was possible.

"I must be dreaming," he said aloud.

He reached down and pinched the back of his left hand.

"Ouch!" he exclaimed, as he swiftly pulled his hand away and waved it back and forth in the air.

"Nope. Not dreaming," he concluded. "Maybe I am just losing it."

Alex looked around more slowly this time, and studied his new surroundings. He found himself to be in an open field near a dirt road. The field was lush and green, and there were small animals and insects of all kinds moving about: rabbits, squirrels, grasshoppers and butterflies, just to name a few. Trees lined the sides of the nearby road, and the sun was brightly shining high up in the blue skies above. If he had to take a guess at what the time of day was, he would have to say it was somewhere around early afternoon.

After looking around the immediate area, he turned his attention to himself and looked down at his clothes. He noticed that he was no longer wearing his pajamas. Instead, he was wearing an outfit that resembled costumes he once saw at a Renaissance Fair he went to with his mother. The ensemble he wore was like what a nobleman would wear, rather than commoner or peasants' clothes. The pants and coat were made of a fine burgundy satin-like cloth and had some sort of metal buttons. The high-collared shirt he wore was pleated down the center and had ruffles around the cuffs.

"Where the heck did these come from," he asked himself.

Alex turned his thoughts away from his costume and decided to explore the land around him. His mind could not make sense of how any of these events were even possible; the hallway, his clothing, the world before him. The last he recalled, before any of this started, was being in his bed trying to fall asleep.

He walked across the open field, stopped at the side of the dirt road and looked in both directions. He looked off to the left, but nothing was there. Then he turned his gaze to the right. Off in the distance, he saw that a rider was approaching on horseback. As the rider grew closer and closer to him, he could see that the rider was in fact, a knight.

The knight saw the young boy standing at the side of the road, and he slowed his horse. Finally, when he was next to Alex, the knight pulled back on the reins, and brought the mighty beast to a stop.

The knight was outfitted in a complete set of silver armour. His shield bore the crest of a griffin, with a spear gripped in one talon and a sword in the other. He raised the visor on his helmet and revealed a man with gentle green eyes. Alex was unsure what to make of what he was seeing, but he was not frightened by the knight.

"Good Day to you, Sir. I am Lord Deker. Captain of the Guard and Knight to their Royal Highnesses who govern these lands."

"Good Day to you, my Lord. I am Alexander. I am searching for my mother. Her name is Sarah. Have you seen her? She is a beautiful woman with long curly blond hair and big blue eyes like mine."

Lord Deker removed his helmet and revealed a kind face to go along with the gentle eyes. He had a full beard that was neatly trimmed. His dark brown hair was somewhat long and straight.

Lord Deker sighed and answered, "Alas, Young Alexander, I have not. I too am in search of someone. I am on a quest to find a strange little man who is said to have a camp somewhere nearby in these woods. Have you, in your travels, seen anyone like that?"

"No, I am sorry, my Lord," answered Alex. "I have not. I only arrived here a short time ago. Who is this man you search for?"

"He is a vile little creature that the Queen is indebted to for reasons of which I am not aware. But for payment of past services to my Queen, he has laid claim to her first-born child. When the Queen refused to give up her child, the strange little man offered her a challenge, instead. He told her she had three nights in which to discover his name. If she succeeded, she would be able to keep her child. Should she fail, then the child would be forever his. Once he left the palace, the Queen dispatched all of the knights and messengers from the kingdom to search for and find out the name of this dreadful little imp in the hopes that she could keep her child."

Alex could not help but notice a familiarity in the tale told by Lord Deker. He knew it to be the story of *Rumpelstiltskin*. His mother, Sarah, read it to him just the other night.

"Perhaps I can help you in your quest to find this man and together, we can learn his name," offered Alex.

"I would welcome your assistance and companionship, young Master Alexander."

Lord Deker secured his helmet to the side of his saddle, then he reached down his arm, offering it to Alex. He pulled the boy up onto his horse. Lord Deker explained that there was a small village nearby and together they rode on towards it.

"So, young Master Alexander, tell me about the place from whence you came."

"I come from a land far from here, my Lord." answered Alex. "By day, I attend to my studies. I really like math and reading. When my schooling is done for the day, I go home where I watch over my mother. She tells me I am the 'man of the house.'"

"What of your father?" Lord Deker asked.

"My father was ill for a very long time. He went to be with God in Heaven a couple of years ago. I miss him dearly."

"I am truly sorry for your loss, my young friend. It is not easy to lose a father at such a young age. He must have been a good man."

Alex nodded and said, "Yes, he was, but how could you know what kind of man he was, having never met him?"

Lord Deker answered, "I do not need to meet a man to know what he is like. I see in you a kindness and honesty that can only come from having a good man as your father, teacher and role model. You are a reflection of your father's ways, his legacy."

"Thank you for your kind words, my Lord," said Alex. "My mother tells me that I am very much my father's son."

Lord Deker smiled at his young companion.

The two rode on for another hour or so until they reached the small settlement. There was little activity happening along the main road. Lord Deker dismounted his steed and helped young Alex down. The villagers watched cautiously from their windows, as the unlikely pair looked for a place to tie up the horse. Lord Deker found a post near a small barn that served as the village stables and tied the horse's reins to it. Slowly, the villagers came out from their homes and gathered near the village square. They were curious to find out why a knight was here in their home place.

As Lord Deker and Alex walked towards the crowd of people, they parted the way, and an older bearded man stepped forward. He had short dark hair that was thinning on the top. Patches of gray on the sides added to his distinguishing features. His brown eyes looked to the knight and his young companion with curiosity. The knight and the young boy stopped before him.

"Good day to you, my Lord. I am the village elder, Reese. I speak for the people you see gathered here before you. How may we be of service to you and your companion?" he asked.

The knight replied, "Good day to you, Elder Reese." Then he leaned in towards the village leader and whispered, "With your permission, good sir, I wish to address the people of your village."

Elder Reese bowed and nodded, "Of course, my Lord."

Lord Deker returned the gesture of respect to the village leader, then turned and spoke to the gathering of villagers.

"Good day to you all. I am Lord Deker, Knight of the Kingdom and Captain of His Majesty's Royal Guard. My comrade, young

Master Alexander, and I are on a quest. We seek any and all information that will aid us in finding a strange little man said to have set up his camp somewhere in the woods nearby. If any of you have seen such a man, your knowledge and assistance to the Crown would be greatly appreciated."

Elder Reese looked around for any indication from his people that they might have seen the little man of whom the knight was speaking. When there were none, he turned back to Alex and Lord Deker and said, "I apologize, my Lord. It does not appear that anyone here has seen such a man. If you desire, I can dispatch some of my people to search the countryside for you."

Lord Deker bowed in thanks to village leader, "It would be greatly appreciated, Elder Reese. If they should happen to find the man we seek, they should not approach him. He may be dangerous. Instead, they should come back here and send forth a messenger to the castle and alert the Guard. My men will know what is to be done."

Reese motioned for one of his men to come forth. The young man stepped over to Elder Reese's side.

"My Lord, this is Jhaden. He is our best and bravest scout, and he is very skillful at tracking, not to mention his expertise when handling a bow, a blade or a horse. If anyone can find your little man, it is he."

Lord Deker took a quick moment to study the young man standing before him. He had short-cropped, dark brown hair and a closely trimmed beard. His hazel-colored eyes had a playful, almost mischievous gaze to them. His body was trim and fit, and his confident bearing made him seem taller than his actual height. The

Knight Captain concluded that Jhaden was not a man to be taken lightly in a serious situation.

Lord Deker nodded to the young man. "Thank you, Jhaden."

"I will do my best to find the man you seek, my Lord" replied Jhaden.

Jhaden looked down at Alex, ruffled his hair and winked at the young lad. Alex smiled back at him.

Then Lord Deker turned back to the village leader and said, "My thanks to you and your people for your willingness to lend a hand, Elder Reese."

Reese returned the bow and replied, "It is our pleasure to serve both you, and the Crown, my Lord."

Elder Reese then turned to the men of his village and said, "Any able-bodied man willing to help, come forth. We shall be assisting Lord Deker in his search of the surrounding areas. For those of you with pack mules or dray horses, you will be assigned the outer regions. The others without mounts, will search the areas closer in to the village. Heed Lord Deker's warning not to approach this man they seek. Should you find him, make your way back here, and we will send forth a messenger to the palace."

With their orders given, the men of the village all nodded, acknowledging they understood Elder Reese's instructions. They spoke quietly amongst themselves with Jhaden, who had taken charge of the search party.

Jhaden bent over and picked up a stick. He then knelt down and began drawing a map of the area in the dirt. He divided the countryside up into search areas and assigned one man to each.

When each man knew his assigned area, the ones with mounts left to fetch them. Those without, started walking towards their designated search area. The mounted villagers climbed on their animals and rode off into the surrounding woods.

Jhaden left the village square only to reappear a few minutes later, leading a beautiful black horse. He made one final check of his steed and equipment, then he mounted up and rode out west from the village.

Alex watched as Jhaden departed. Like Elder Reese said, the man knew how to ride a horse. He and the beast seemed to move as one as they rode off along the trails leading up into the hills.

Lord Deker watched, as well. He found it strange that Jhaden, a commoner, owned such a fine steed. He turned to Elder Reese with a puzzling look, but before he could ask the question, Reese explained.

"Jhaden has been with us for several years now. He came here seeking a new, simpler life. He was once a soldier from another kingdom far from this place, where a ruthless tyrant ruled. His morals were in conflict with his King, and they would not allow him to serve under such a corrupt dictator. He resigned from his commission as a soldier and left. His horse, weapons and equipment are all that remains from his life before coming here. He is a brave and honorable man, of the highest caliber." Reese paused a moment then smiled, "Though sometimes, he can be a bit mischievous."

"Sounds like a good man to have around when things go awry."

"Yes, he is. I would not think twice about trusting him with my life or the lives of anyone dear to me."

Lord Deker smiled at Reese's confidence in the young man's abilities and integrity, "Then I shall trust him, too."

When the last villager from the search party disappeared from sight, Lord Deker looked to Alex and said, "It is time for us to move on and continue our own search."

They turned and walked from the village square towards the village stable, where Lord Deker's horse was tied. The knight mounted his horse, then he extended his arm down to Alex and helped him back up onto the beast.

Before turning to leave, Lord Deker looked to Elder Reese. He placed his right hand over his heart and bowed his head in thanks to the village leader. The remaining villagers, in turn, bowed to the knight and his friend, as they began to ride off continuing their journey.

"I wish you luck in your quest, my Lord," called out Elder Reese, as he waved to the noble knight and his companion.

"Thank you, sir," replied the knight, returning the wave.

Alex looked up to Lord Deker and said, "I liked Jhaden."

Lord Deker smiled, "As did I. He looks to be a good man."

The two left the small village behind, riding to the north. After hours of finding no evidence of a campsite, they then turned westward. Occasionally, they came upon one of the men from the village. Each shook their head as Lord Deker passed by, indicating they had had no luck in finding the little man's campsite, yet.

The two continued onward.

Jhaden rode his steed along the bluffs overlooking the river that provided water to his village. He reasoned that if the little man had setup a campsite, the most likely place would have to be somewhere close to the water.

He stopped from time to time and pulled out his spyglass to search the surrounding area. When he found nothing, he put the small telescope away and continued his search.

In time, he came upon a well-traveled path as he rode his horse down from the bluffs. There, he spotted a set of fresh small hoof prints and what looked to be the tracks from a wagon or cart of some sort leading up to the river's edge. Someone had recently stopped there to water their mount.

He jumped down from his horse and examined the tracks more closely. Among the hoof prints and wheel marks was a small set of foot prints, about the size a child would make. Knowing that children would not be allowed to go out and about on their own, he concluded these tracks had to have been made by the little man.

A second set of prints near the first were deeper in the earth, as if someone had pushed off from the ground while climbing back up onto the wagon or cart. The wheel tracks and the hoof prints then turned and continued on upstream along the trail next to the river.

Jhaden began to follow them, carefully and quietly. Wherever possible, he used the trees and brush that lined the shoreline of the river for cover. The terrain before him then split into two. The tracks from the wagon continued on the lower trail next to the edge of the river, but Jhaden decided to take the higher ground. From this vantage point above, he could follow the tracks below and still maintain his covert search.

He followed the tracks for a few minutes longer, looking and listening along the way for any signs of the little man's campsite. Suddenly, he heard a commotion coming from somewhere up ahead. He dismounted his horse and tied the reins off to a nearby tree. Once his horse was secure, Jhaden crept up to the edge of the bluffs where the thick bushes would provide him cover.

The commotion seemed to be coming from across the river, where there was a clearing in the woods. He pulled out his spyglass again and trained it on the area whence the sounds were coming.

There, he spotted a small man, who was bent over a pile of wood. He appeared to be making a campfire. Jhaden could hear the little man talking to himself though he could not make out what he was saying. Then, all at once, the little man started laughing out loud, as if he had just heard the funniest joke ever told. When he settled back down from his fit of laughter, he returned to the task of building his fire and talking to himself.

Jhaden searched the area around the campsite and noticed a trail just up river that led up to the water's edge. The river there, looked shallow enough to cross. He scouted the opposite shoreline with his spyglass and noticed a dense enough tree and brush cover that could be used to sneak up on the campsite without being seen.

Jhaden then backed away from the edge of the bluffs and backtracked to where his horse was tied. As quietly as possible, he untied the horse and led it away from the river. When he was far enough from the river, he climbed upon his steed and snapped his reins. The beast charged forward and raced off towards the trail near the river.

Several hours had passed since Alex and Lord Deker had met with the villagers. The sun was beginning to set on the distant hills. The long day was coming to an end.

Lord Deker looked down towards Alex and said, "We should find someplace and make camp for the night. We can get a fresh start in the morning."

They rode on searching for a suitable place to set up a campsite.

Suddenly, Alex noticed something off in the distance. A dust cloud rose up from the road, signaling that a rider was fast approaching. Alex tapped on Lord Deker's forearm and pointed at the road ahead. "Someone is coming this way," he said.

As the rider neared, he saw Lord Deker and Alex. He began to pull back on his reins and slow his steed, bringing it to a halt in front of the knight and his companion. The young rider, appearing out of breath, bowed to Lord Deker. It was Jhaden.

"My Lord. I was riding back to the village to report in."

"At the speed in which you were riding, young Jhaden, I suspect that you have found something," said Lord Deker.

"Yes, my Lord. I believe I found the man you seek. His campsite is about an hour's ride down this road. You will come to a fork in the road. Take the left one. Ride on for another few minutes, and you will see a large oak tree by the roadside. There is a trail there. Turn left on the trail, and it will lead you to a river. When you arrive at the river, the little man's campsite is on the opposite shore just downstream from your position. The river is shallow enough to cross where the trail leads into the water and the trees and brush are dense enough to hide your approach."

"Thank you, young Jhaden. Elder Reese was right about your skills as a tracker. Your service to the Kingdom and to me shall not be overlooked. Ride on to your village and inform Elder Reese of what you have found. Young Alexander and I will continue on towards the little man's camp. There is no need to send a messenger to the castle. I will take it from here."

Jhaden nodded and bowed to the knight. "Of course, my Lord. I am your humble servant."

Lord Deker smiled, then he extended his hand and said, "Again, my thanks to you, Jhaden. If ever, you should desire to join the castle guard and become one of my men, seek me out at the palace. I can always use a good man like you."

"Thank you, my Lord. You are most gracious," replied the young scout accepting the knight's hand as a gesture of friendship.

Alex smiled, "Good bye, Jhaden. It was nice to meet you."

"Good bye, Alexander. Safe travels to you, my young friend."

"And you, as well."

Jhaden turned and snapped his reins. His horse leapt forward once again, heading home, towards his village. Lord Deker, in turn, snapped his, and his own horse sprinted off down the road in the direction from whence Jhaden had come. Alex hung on to the knight for dear life, as the horse raced on.

Another hour passed, and they finally came to the fork in the road. Lord Deker expertly guided his horse to the left. Within minutes, Alex spotted the large oak tree of which Jhaden had spoken. He pointed it out. Lord Deker slowed his steed and turned left onto the trail that would take them to the river. The night was now dark, and the air was cool. They followed the trail, until they could see the heavily wooded bank of the river.

Lord Deker dismounted his horse and walked to the river's edge, careful to stay concealed in the trees and brush that lined its bank. He looked downstream and could see the faint flickering light of a camp fire. The quiet night air carried a distant sound of someone in the direction of the campsite.

Lord Deker walked back to the side of his horse and helped Alex off of the mighty steed. Keeping the boy in his arms, he carried Alex across the shallow part of the river.

Once on the other side, he put Alex down and together, they used the trees as cover to get closer to the campsite. They both moved cautiously and quietly to maintain their stealthy approach. The light from the campfire grew brighter the closer they got to it.

As they reached the perimeter of the campsite, Alex carefully pushed aside the branches of the brush trees and looked through. There, he saw a clearing surrounded by trees. At the center of the clearing was a small tent with a roaring campfire at its side. There was a small wagon next to the tent and a pony was tied off to rear of the wagon.

Around the campfire danced a strange and funny little man. As he danced about, he was banging on a pot with a wooden spoon and singing a crude off-tune jingle.

"Tomorrow I'll brew, today I bake, and then the child away I'll take. The Royal Queen will never guess that Rothrendorstein is my name!"

The little man stopped to laugh out loudly, then he repeated his song and continued his dance around the campfire.

Alex took a moment to listen to the words of the song again, thinking he might have misheard what the little man sang the first time. When the song ended for the second time, he confirmed that he heard the same words he thought he heard the first. This was confusing to him.

"Rothrendorstein? That's not the right name," he thought to himself. Lord Deker did not see the puzzling look on Alex's face. He quietly motioned to Alex that they had what they came for and that it was time for them to leave.

"Come, young Alexander," he whispered. "We now know the name of the little man. We must make our way back to the palace and tell the Queen what we have learned."

The two quietly backed away from the little man's campsite and made their way back to the river's edge. Lord Deker again carried Alex across. Once on the other side, Alex was helped back up onto the horse, and Lord Deker led the beast away from the river. When they were far enough away, the knight mounted up. With a snap of his reins, the horse charged forward, speeding off in the direction of the castle.

As Lord Deker and Alex disappeared around a bend, the campsite suddenly erupted into bursts of charged electrical energy. Arcs of lightning lashed out at the campsite, striking the tent and campfire, causing them to disappear. The small wagon and pony faded away from existence. Everything from the campsite vanished without a trace, as if they were never there.

The little man then walked to the center of the clearing. He began to laugh again. It was an evil sort of laugh, and it grew louder and more ominous with each passing moment.

Suddenly, the little man was engulfed in fire and black smoke. As the smoke cleared, a dark figure was revealed, dressed from head to toe in black; a black so dark it rivaled the night sky. He raised his arms up towards the half-moon, high up in the heavens. The sleeves from his cloak raised just enough to reveal his hands and forearms. The skin was pale. So pale that it looked as if he had little or no blood flowing through his veins. His cold black eyes burned with an unspeakable hatred as he looked off in the direction of the castle. Then, he moved his lips to speak.

"So much for the Queens's happy ending," he said, and he began to laugh yet again, louder and louder. The nearby animals scurried off in all directions, looking for a place to hide from the sound of the hideous glee. The night air grew deathly silent except for the movements of the dark-cloaked figure. He reached down and grabbed the edge of his black cloak and pulled it upwards and around him. He spun around and a dark cloud of smoke enveloped him. As the black smoke dissipated, the shadowy man had vanished, without leaving a trace that he was ever there.

Alex and Lord Deker rode on throughout the night. At dawn, a castle appeared off in the distance. The palace sat on a small island and was surrounded by water on all sides. Lord Deker steered his mount up to the lowered drawbridge of the palace and slowed the galloping beast down to a trot as they crossed over the moat waters below. Once on the other side of the bridge, he coaxed his horse towards the stables, and there, he helped Alex down, then he dismounted the horse, himself.

"We must see the Queen, at once," he informed a nearby palace sentry, who snapped to attention and saluted. "At once, my Lord."

Lord Deker returned the salute.

He then turned to the stable boy, handed him the reins to his mount and said, "Please see to my horse and take good care of him." Lord Deker stroked the side of his beloved horse as he spoke. "Give him extra fodder. He has earned it. We have both had a long and hard journey."

The stable boy nodded and replied, "Yes, my Lord. I will see to it myself, immediately."

Lord Deker turned to Alex and said, "Come with me, young Master Alexander. The Queen awaits us."

The sentry escorted Lord Deker into the castle. Alex followed behind them, almost running to keep up with the knight's quickened pace. They walked swiftly down a series of hallways.

When they arrived at the throne room, the two guardsmen standing post on either side of the entrance snapped to attention and saluted their Captain. Lord Deker returned the salute of his men and walked into the room.

The Queen sat on her throne, holding her newly-born son in her arms. To Alex, she looked like a woman who was deeply troubled, almost as if she had the entire weight of the world on her shoulders. She was petite, and had long brown hair, big hazel-colored eyes and a beauty fitting that of a Queen.

She noticed the sound of someone entering the room and looked up as Lord Deker approached the throne. There was a sudden look of hope in her tear-filled eyes. She waited with anticipation as the knight advanced towards her.

Lord Deker stopped in front of her throne and took a knee. Alex followed suit and kneeled, as well.

"What news, if any, do you bring to me, Captain? Good, I hope."

"I do indeed, your Majesty. I bring you the name in which you seek."

"Oh, thank the heavens. I had just about given up hope, having been awake all night, trying to think of names," she replied. She turned her head slightly and noticed the young boy at Lord Deker's side, kneeling before her.

"And who is this with you?" she asked.

"Your Majesty, may I present young Master Alexander. I happened across him during my journey. He has become separated from his mother, and I could not, in all good conscience, leave him alone in the woods. He has provided me with company during my quest, and together, we found the little man's campsite."

"Alexander, this is Her Royal Highness, Queen Catherine."

"It is an honor to meet you, young Alexander," said the Queen.

"The honor is mine, your Majesty."

The Queen turned her attention back to the knight kneeling before her. She motioned for them both to stand. Lord Deker and Alex rose up as the Queen asked, "So, Lord Deker, what is the name that you bring me?"

"My Queen, young Alexander and I rode into a nearby village where the leader, a man named Reese, offered to send out search parties into the countryside to look for the little man's campsite. Alexander and I rode on, continuing our own search. At sunset, we happened to come across one of the men, who had been dispatched from the village. He was riding hard and fast back towards his home. This young man's name was Jhaden. He reported to us that he had spotted the little man's campsite near the river. I sent young Jhaden on towards his home and rode out to where he said the camp was located. Young Alexander and I found the campsite, and we watched the little man, hoping to learn his name. He was dancing around a campfire and singing a curious song. The lyrics he sang spoke of taking your child from you and that you would never guess that his name was *Rothrendorstein*."

When she heard the name she sought being spoken aloud, Queen Catherine let out a great sigh of relief. After a moment of silent and thankful prayer, she turned to a nearby servant girl.

"Emagine," she called out to her.

The servant girl stepped forward and bowed before the Queen, awaiting her orders. "Yes, My Queen?"

"Go to the kitchen and tell the cooks to make preparations for a grand celebration. Lord Deker and young Master Alexander are to be honored for completing their mission and bringing me the name of the man who wants to take my child from me."

"Your Majesty," Lord Deker interrupted. "A celebration to honor us is not necessary. Moreover, it was young Jhaden who actually found the little man's campsite. It is he, who should receive your thanks and praise. I was only doing my duty."

"Nonsense," she countered. "You are to be commended for your brave and noble service to me, Captain. I owe you a great debt of gratitude for what you have done. A celebration is the least that I can do. Besides, I will see to it that Jhaden, Reese and the people of their village are properly rewarded for their actions on this day." She then nodded to the servant girl to carry out her wishes.

The young woman again bowed to the Queen and said, "At once, my Queen." Emagine then turned and left the throne room, heading towards the kitchen to see to the planning of a celebration.

Hours later, the festivities of the celebration were in full swing. The air was filled with the sounds of music and of people joyfully laughing. The dance floor bustled with merriment as the guests danced in celebration. The King's Fool toured throughout the crowd entertaining everyone with his hijinks, making the onlookers laugh even louder.

Alex and Lord Deker sat in a place of honor at a grand table located on a dais at the head of the room. Many of the people attending the celebration stopped by their table to congratulate the two on successfully completing the Queen's mission. Lord Deker seemed almost embarrassed by all the attention being bestowed upon him. In his mind, he was doing his duty and all of the celebration and accolades in his honor seemed unnecessary.

Finally, there was a lull in the flood of well-wishers stopping by their table. Alex turned towards Lord Deker and asked, "So what is it like to be a knight?"

The noble knight pondered the young lad's question for a moment, smiled, and then answered, "It is not just about honor, but about loyalty and serving their Majesties. If I were called upon to do so, I would gladly lay down my life for those whom I serve. I am here to protect the kingdom and its subjects against any foe who would see harm done to it. I ask no questions. I only do my duty."

"Yeah, but you did not even know why the Queen wanted you to learn the little man's name. How could you know it was the right thing to do?"

"It is not my place to question the needs of my Queen. It is my place to do her bidding," insisted Lord Deker.

"So, what if she asked you to do something bad?" asked Alex.

"As you get older, Alexander, you will learn to better understand how to judge these things. I know the woman, who is my Queen," he replied. "She is both a good-hearted person and a kind ruler. She would never ask me or my men to do something that went against the laws of man. Were she not an honorable woman, or if I were asked to carry out an evil act, then yes, I might question my orders. But, my Queen is noble and true. I am now, and forever will be, her faithful servant."

"Wow! I wish I had even a small amount of your courage, Lord Deker."

"Why do you say that, Young Alexander?"

"Where I come from, some of the children there think of me as weak and scared. Because of this, they torment me constantly. If I were as brave as you, I could stand up to the worst of them so that the others would see that I am not a coward."

"Ah, my young friend, I was not always the brave and gallant knight you see before you. Like you, I was once a boy, and like you, I was once faced by those who taunted me. You are braver than you think. One day, I will have to tell you of my life's story and what I had to overcome to be the man I am today."

Suddenly, there was a commotion at the back of the ballroom. The doors flew open and the strange little man walked in. The people were startled by his appearance, and everyone parted the way, as he walked through the crowd towards the Queen.

Alex noticed that he, himself, was taller than the little man. His skin was wrinkled from the passage of time. Were he not there to take the Queen's child from her, someone might mistakenly think him frail.

Lord Deker rose up from his table and his men stood close by, ready to spring into action, at the start of any trouble. Many of the guardsman already had their hands on the grips of their swords, prepared to draw, and defend the Crown.

"A party!" said the little man, excitedly. "And I was not even invited? I am so wounded by this." The little man feigned as if his feelings were hurt and then burst into a loud and eerie laughter. He continued onward towards the throne, making his way through the crowd. He stopped before the Queen, and he bowed to her in jest, rather than respect.

"Your Majesty," he said, then he burst into another fit of evil laughter.

"You are an evil and wretched little man," the Queen remarked.

"Sticks and stones may break my bones," he replied.

"I should have my guards arrest you and take you to the dungeon," she countered. "You are a man without honor nor conscience."

"Come now," he said, turning his eyes towards the guards, standing close by, daring them to act. "Do you really think that your guards would have the ability to take me on? How soon you have forgotten what my powers did for you. These guards of yours would know defeat before they even made their first move."

Lord Deker moved away from his table to position himself between the little man and the Queen. His sword was already half drawn.

"Show the respect befitting a Queen, you little toad," he challenged angrily.

The little man stopped and turned his attention to Lord Deker.

"And who might you be?"

"I am Lord Deker, Knight Captain of his Majesty's Royal Guard and sworn protector of this kingdom."

"Wow! That is a mouthful," he teased. "Be careful, Captain," the little man cautioned. "For if you do not, I will surely strike you down."

Lord Deker replied, "If taking down an evil soul such as yourself results in my death, I would gladly give my life in service to my kingdom."

"Oh! How noble of you, my dear, brave, Captain. Your courage is very commendable," taunted the little man. "Or very stupid." Then he laughed, again.

Lord Deker became flushed with anger. He tightened his grip on his sword and prepared to draw.

Queen Catherine took a step forward and placed her hand on Lord Deker's shoulder, silently asking him to stand down. She smiled at him and then looked to the little man and said, "Your evil ways will not prevail."

"Well then, straight to the business at hand. Tonight is your last night to guess my name, my dear. Should you fail, then I will take my prize, and you will never see me nor your child, again."

"We will see about that," said the Queen defiantly.

"Ooh! Feisty. Aren't we?" the little man replied in a most rude manner. He looked to an angry Lord Deker as he continued. "So, Madame Queen, what is my name?"

"Is your name Conrad?" she asked.

"No."

"Is it Harry or Samuel?"

"No, and no," he replied. "If you have no other guess, I will be off with the child."

"Well, let me see." The Queen smiled. "It is not Timothy?"

"No," he replied.

"Perhaps William, Sheepshanks, Cruickshanks or Spindleshanks?" she asked.

"No. No. No. No," he replied again.

She paused a moment as if she were thinking real hard.

The little man stood by impatiently. "Time is a wasting," he said.

Finally, she smiled and said, "Then maybe it is Rothrendorstein."

"Wrong again!" he gleefully exclaimed.

A sudden look of terror filled the Queen's eyes. She looked to Lord Deker who was stunned. He was certain of what he had heard, as he watched the little man dance around the campfire the night before. He turned and looked over to Alex for some sign of confirmation. Alex just stood there, puzzled by the drama unfolding before him. Lord Deker turned back to the Queen.

"My Queen, I swear to you. That is the name I heard. He is lying."

The little man stepped closer to where the Queen was standing. He held out his hands, waiting for the Queen to present him with his reward. The Queen turned away, shielding her child from the little man. The newly born baby began to cry. She took a step forward as if she were ready to sprint away.

"Come now, Your Majesty. I won, fair and square," he cautioned. "Do you wish to put your people at further risk from my wrath? Do you want them to suffer for your unwillingness to honor our deal? For I will lay waste to this kingdom and make it burn like all Hades, if I am denied my prize. Their fate now lies in your hands."

She hesitated; unsure what to do. How could anyone ask a mother to give up her child? Yet, how could she ask her people to sacrifice their lives in return for a desperate promise she had made.

It seemed like a lifetime ago, but in reality, it had only been a little over a year.

She was once just plain old Catherine, the daughter of a poor miller. Her father, who often drank too much at the local village tavern, frequently boasted to anyone who would listen, about how beautiful his daughter was. One day, as fate would have it, he was granted an audience with the King.

The miller was a common man, and like many, he had ambitions of becoming an important person. To make himself sound more important than he really was, he declared to the King that his own daughter had the power to spin common straw into gold.

The King, who was known for his love of gold, told the miller to bring his daughter to the palace, so that she could be put to the test. The miller never expected the King to ask this of him, but he did as he was ordered, rather than expose himself to all for the liar he was.

Catherine was brought before the King, and he in turn led her to a room full of straw. There, inside, at the center of the room was a spinning wheel and spindle. He told her to spin all of the straw into gold by morning, for if she could not, she would surely die. The King closed the door behind him and locked it.

Catherine was unsure how to do what the King had asked of her. She suddenly feared for her life. Overwhelmed by her current predicament, she sank to the floor and began to cry. How could her father have put her in this position? What was he thinking? She could hardly believe this was happening to her. What was she to do?

Just then, the tumbler on the locked door clicked. The door swung open and in walked a tiny little man, not more than three feet tall. He was old and wrinkled, with hair as white as snow, and there was a mischievous gleam in his eyes. He saw the young maiden sitting there on the floor crying, so he asked her what was the matter. Catherine told the little man all about the story of her father's claims to the King, and how she was now asked to spin all of the straw before them into gold. She professed to the little man that she had no idea how to do what her father had claimed, and if she could not do so by morning, she would surely loose her life.

The little man laughed and said he could help her with her precarious circumstance, but he wanted something in return. Catherine thought for a moment, then she offered him her necklace. He took the necklace from her and looked it over, then he agreed and set himself to work, spinning the straw into gold. After a time, Catherine grew tired and fell asleep.

By morning, the little man's task was complete, and he vanished, as though he was never there. The young maiden awoke to the sound of the enormous wooden door being unlocked.

The King walked into a room full of gold where there was once straw. He was giddy with delight at the sight of all the gold before him, but his lust for the prized metal was too much. He decreed that she would spend another night in another room and spin more straw into gold.

Later that night, just like the night before, Catherine was led to a room and locked in. And just as before, she began to cry, unsure how to proceed. This room was larger than the last, and it had twice as much straw as the one yesterday.

As it happened the night before, the locked door opened up and the little man walked in. He asked the young Catherine what she would give him this time to spin the room full of straw into gold. This time, she offered him the ring from her finger. The little man agreed, took the ring from her, and began his work. He spun throughout the night and by morning the room was full of gold, then he disappeared without a trace.

At dawn, the King again unlocked the door and came into the room. He was filled with astonishment and delight at the sight of his favorite thing, but his greed's thirst had still not been quenched. He then declared the miller's daughter was to be put into the largest room in the castle, and it would be filled to the top with straw. If she could spin all of this into gold, he would make her his wife.

So like the two preceding nights, she was taken to a room full of straw and locked in, and like the two nights before, she began to cry. Again, the little man appeared and asked her what she would give him in return for his services. This time, though, she told him she had nothing left to give. He thought for a moment then said he would gladly accept her first-born child as payment, once she became Queen. With nothing else to give and no one else to turn to, she reluctantly agreed.

In the morning, the King found the room filled with gold and without a moment's hesitation, he kept his promise to marry the miller's daughter. Catherine was now Queen.

One year later, a son was born to the King and Queen. She was so happy with how her life had turned out that she had all but forgotten of her debt to the little man.

Then one day, the little man suddenly appeared and demanded his payment. The Queen was surprised by his return. Not wanting to lose her son, she offered the little man all of the riches in the kingdom in exchange for the debt she owed him.

The little imp declined her offer of compensation and the Queen began to cry. A moment later he offered her a glimmer of hope. A challenge; with three chances for her to keep her son. He gave her three days in which to learn his name. If she guessed correctly, the debt would be satisfied, and she would keep her child. If not, then the boy would leave with him and she would never see him again.

She spent the first night thinking of and calling out all of the common names she had ever heard, but none of those were the name she needed. In desperation, she sent forth messengers and knights, including Lord Deker, out into the kingdom to search for and learn the name of the little man.

The second night did not go well for the Queen, either. This night, she called off all of the uncommon names she could think of. Still none of these were the name she needed.

When Lord Deker appeared with Alex earlier on that third day with what was believed to be the name of the little man, she thought she would be able to keep her son. Suddenly, she felt alone and utterly lost.

"I'm waiting," said the little man, his hands still stretched out in anticipation of his prize.

She began to cry out frantically. "No! Please. I beg of you. Do not take my child from me."

"A deal is a deal," he replied as he laughed.

Two of the palace guards advanced on the little man with their swords drawn. With a wave of his hand, they were thrown backwards and collided against the stone wall. They crumpled to the floor, unconscious. Another guard prepared to approach and subdue the little man, but the Queen cried out, "Stop!"

The guards halted their approach.

Queen Catherine looked down at her newborn son, then upwards at her people who had gathered before her. She knew all too well what the little man was capable of. Indeed, he had the power to do as he had threatened; to punish her people and lay waste to the kingdom.

"I cannot put everyone's lives in danger by failing to keep a desperate promise I made to this man." She turned to Lord Deker and said, "Have your men stand down, Captain."

"Are you certain, my Queen?" he asked. "My men and I will fight to the very last of us if that be your wish."

"It is the only way to ensure the safety of the kingdom," she said.

Lord Deker's shoulders sank, as he waived his men off and they backed away from the little man.

The Queen kissed her baby son on the forehead and whispered into his tiny ear, "Mother loves you, my sweet, precious son. Always remember that."

She turned back to face the little man and slowly placed her infant son into his waiting hands. She then sank to the floor and began to weep. The little man turned and began to leave, laughing as he walked away.

Alex was still confused by what had just happened. "This just isn't right," he said silently to himself. "This is not how it is supposed to go. I have to do something. I have to make things right."

He then pushed his way through the crowd of onlookers and rushed to the side of the distraught Queen. He pulled her towards him and placed his hand on her opposite cheek, drawing her close enough so that he could whisper into her ear. "Rumpelstiltskin. His name is Rumpelstiltskin."

The Queen turned and peered into Alex's eyes. There, she saw an innocence and truth in those young eyes. After hearing Alex's words, she stopped crying and composed herself. With the assistance of Alex, she stood up and turned towards the little man, who was nearing the door.

"Wait! You twisted little snake!" she called out angrily.

The little man stopped and turned back to her. "Yes?" he said. "You have something else to add before I leave?"

"Yes I do," she replied defiantly. "Your name...Your name is Rumpelstiltskin."

The little man's cold gray eyes grew wide with surprise. The veins in his forehead began to throb with anger. Stunned by what he had just heard, he staggered unsteadily forward towards the center of the room.

"What!" he cried out. "Who told you? This is not fair!"

Fearing for the safety of the young Prince, Lord Deker moved in towards the little man and took the infant from him. He returned the child to the security of his mother, who waited with anxious, outstretched arms. She kissed and hugged her son.

Rumpelstiltskin's shock turned to anger as he continued to rant uncontrollably around the room. The people backed away from the outbursts of the crazed little man.

"Some demon has told you has told you my name. You cheated."

Rumpelstiltskin became angrier and began to stomp on the floor. A vortex of bright white light suddenly appeared all around him and swallowed him up. Then the light faded away and disappeared, taking with it any sign of the little man.

Lord Deker turned his attention towards Alex, who was still at the Queen's side. He knelt down on one knee, coming eye to eye with the young hero.

"Thank you, young Master Alexander," he said gratefully, as he placed his hand over his heart and bowed his head. "You have saved the day, and you have defended my Queen and this kingdom with honor against a most contemptible foe."

"Yes. Yes," agreed the Queen. "Thank you, Alexander. If not for you, I would not have my son in my arms. You shall forever be welcome in this kingdom for as long as I shall live."

The Queen kissed her child on the forehead once again and handed him over to the servant girl, Emagine. She turned and walked towards the King, who was standing by his throne. She drew his sword, turned back towards the crowd and held the blade up in a ceremonial pose.

"Come forth, young Alexander," she said.

Alex walked towards the thrones of the King and Queen. Lord Deker fell in behind. They stopped before the Queen.

"Kneel before me and receive a gesture of my thanks," she commanded.

Alex did as he was told and took a knee before the Queen.

The Queen brought the blade of the sword down to rest on Alex's right shoulder and asked, "Do you, Alexander, promise to protect the lands of this kingdom and its people?"

"I do," he replied.

The Queen raised the blade and placed it on his left shoulder, then asked, "Do you promise that above all else, you will show courage, honor and respect to those whom you serve?"

"I will."

She raised the sword up, turned and handed the blade back to her husband. The King slid it into its sheath.

She turned back to the brave young boy before her. "Then by the powers vested in me as Queen, for your heroic actions on this day, I bestow upon thee the rank of knight. Rise, Sir Alexander."

Alex stood up. He bowed before their Majesties then turned towards the crowd behind him.

Lord Deker began to cheer, and his men followed suit. The cheering became louder and louder as the people joined in. The interrupted celebration started back up and before long, it was in full swing, once again.

Everyone was so distracted by the festivities that nobody noticed the appearance of a door. Nobody that is, except for Alex. It looked to him, exactly like the one that had brought him to this place. The door slowly opened on its own, and Alex walked towards it.

Lord Deker took notice of Alex walking across the room. Then he saw the doorway. Not knowing what it was, he moved towards it cautiously. He called out to Alex, "Wait, Alexander."

Alex turned back to his friend and smiled. "It's Okay, my Lord. It is where I came from. I must continue my search for my Mother."

Lord Deker smiled and said, "I understand, my dear young friend. I wish you good luck and safe travels. Know that if you should ever need me at your side, I will be there."

"Of that, I never had a doubt." Alex bowed to Lord Deker. "You should return to your station at the Queen's side. I am glad I met you. You are a brave and noble knight. I will remember you, always."

Lord Deker bowed in return and said, "As I will you. You are the bravest and kindest young man I have ever met. I hope that someday we will have the pleasure of meeting each other again. Farewell, my dear comrade-in-arms."

Alex smiled at the gallant knight, "Goodbye, Lord Deker."

The knight turned and walked back over to the Queen, while Alex walked to the open door.

He paused for a moment at the threshold, turned and looked back on Lord Deker and Queen Catherine. Both were smiling and both had their happy ending. He smiled, then turned back towards the door and walked through.

Once again, there was a blinding flash of light that appeared and then vanished.

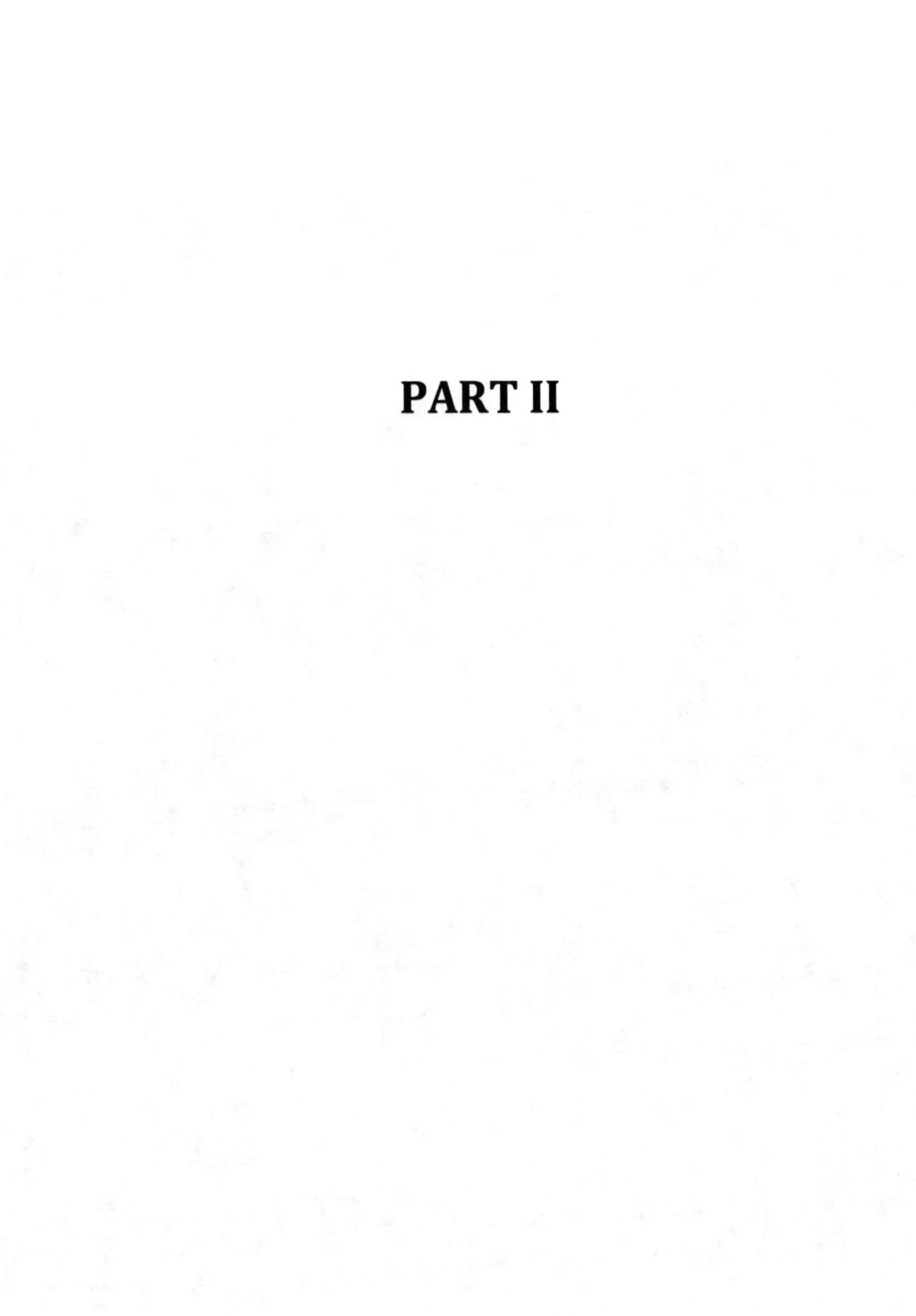

PART II

When the young, recently knighted, Sir Alex's eyes began to adjust to the low lighting, he realized that he had been taken back into the hallway. The door he had walked through to get back here closed behind him.

The passageway was strangely quiet except for the crackling sound of the fire from torches above him and the faint sound of someone breathing. He was not alone. He strained his eyes, trying to make out the silhouetted figure standing in the darkness before him.

"Do not be afraid, Alex," called out a vaguely familiar voice. It came from a woman standing there in the shadows. She stepped forward into the light of a nearby torch, and Alex recognized her immediately, though she did not look the same as the last time he had seen her.

He looked over his shoulder at the door he just came through then turned back towards her. Her face was one of the most beautiful he had ever seen, next to his mother's, of course. She had long, dark, brown hair and her emerald-colored eyes sparkled in the flickering light from the surrounding torches. She wore a long white dress that almost seemed to glow in the ill-lit hallway.

"You are the Queen's servant, Emagine. I just saw you there," he said as he pointed to the door behind him. He had a puzzling look on his face.

"Yes," she replied. "In the story of *Rumpelstiltskin* I was the Queen's servant girl. Here and now, in this place, I am known as the

Lady Emagine, leader of the Council of Tales. I, and the other members of the Council, are the sworn guardians to the tales and legends of mankind. Like you, I only played a part in the story."

"I am pleased to meet you, my Lady," Alex replied as he bowed before her.

Lady Emagine smiled, bowed in return and said, "The pleasure is all mine, Alex, for it is I who brought you here to this place." After a moment, she asked, "Do you know why?"

"No, why?"

"Because you are a very special person," she paused for a brief moment, and, then continued. "There is a great evil that threatens to destroy us all. It grows more powerful with each passing day. To fight that threat, I needed someone who is intelligent enough and well-versed in all of the various stories of mankind. The countless stories your father and mother read to you over the years has made you an expert in this area. I also needed someone who is pure in heart, who can see past the darkness that has plagued these stories, and who can recognize when something is not as it was meant to be. Finally, I needed someone brave. Brave enough not to fear taking action to restore things as they should be."

"When you say recognizing when something was not as it was meant to be, you mean the way I knew things were not right when my mom read *Beauty and the Beast* to me, and when I stopped Rumpelstiltskin from taking Queen Catherine's child away?

"Yes, and more. When you and your mother were talking earlier in the day, you told her how the children at your school behaved differently than normal, even the children who never have gotten into trouble. Then later that night, as she read to you, you noticed that the story of *Beauty and the Beast* did not end as you remembered it. And, in *Rumpelstiltskin*, you knew that the name of the little man that was given to the Queen was not the right one. Believe it or not, all of these events are related to one another. They are all happening at the hands of an evil sorcerer who goes by the name of Nagama."

"Who is this Nagama, and how is he responsible?" asked Alex.

She explained, "Long ago, Nagama was once a good and noble person. Like me, he was a founding member of the Council of Tales. Then, nearly five hundred years ago, I began to notice a change in him. He had always been ambitious in his nature, but eventually, this ambition allowed him to be easily manipulated by some unknown evil force. Time went on and he developed an unquenchable lust for power. As his need for power grew, he began showing nothing but contempt for the mortal man. He believed that we, the immortals of the Council, were better suited to rule over the known world, and that mankind should be subjugated and forced to live under our rule. Eventually, when no one on the Council supported him in his beliefs, he betrayed us. The Council of Tales tried to stop him, but he vanished, escaping to hide somewhere here within the Hall of a Thousand Doors. He has made a vow that he will destroy all the happy endings to the stories you grew up hearing."

"Wait, the Hall of what?" asked Alex.

Lady Emagine started walking down the hallway. Alex followed her. As they walked Lady Emagine continued, "This hallway you find yourself in now, is an enchanted portal. There are one thousand doors here," she said as she pointed in both directions. "Any of these doors, leads to one of a thousand of the most treasured tales of mankind. As you have already seen first-hand, once someone enters a particular doorway, the story comes to life, and they can even interact with the characters from that story."

"And this Council of Tales watches over the hallway?" asked Alex.

"Something like that," she replied. "Since the dawn of man, human beings have told stories to one another. Some of these stories were meant to entertain, while others were meant to teach the lessons of life. Throughout this time of mankind, nations and empires have arisen and fallen. A number of those tales were lost to the devastations of war while others to the passage of time. Then, a little over five-thousand years ago, around 3100 BC, the ancient Sumerians developed the first of many written languages. This new written language was originally intended for use in business and for academics. Four hundred years later though, in 2700 BC, man finally began writing down the first of his stories in order to pass them down from one generation to the next. Still, as man's aggressive, warring ways continued, there were many occasions where a conquering tyrant or dictator destroyed these written tales, because the stories did not fit into his society's way of thinking. This destruction went on for many more years until the year 1443."

Alex listened intently as Lady Emagine continued her history lesson on how the Council came into existence.

"At that time, I, and other magic wielders like myself, lived among mankind. We are what you would call wizards and sorceresses. For the most part, we have tried to stay out of the affairs of mortals, but after so many years of watching countless tales and legends being destroyed or forgotten, I felt that something had to be done to preserve the most significant of these stories. I went to the others and voiced my concerns. We deliberated for some time on what actions we could and should take. Finally, a small group of us decided to ban together to form the Council of Tales. The Council would act as the protectors to these treasured legends. I was elected, by the others, to lead this newly-formed Council. Using our combined magical powers, we then created this enchanted passageway, where the most important stories of mankind could come to life to ensure that they would never perish from history."

Alex took a moment to let what Lady Emagine was telling him sink in, then he asked, "How can Nagama's actions here affect the kids at my school or change the words in my story books?"

"As the happiness in one story dies, it affects all of mankind and changes how your world remembers the story. The more stories touched by Nagama's evil, the more it affects your world. If he succeeds in his quest to destroy the happy endings in all stories, mankind will lose the ability to know happiness." She paused a moment then asked, "Do you recall how your mother reacted when you told her the ending of *Beauty and the Beast* was not how you remembered it; that there was no happy ending?"

Alex nodded as Lady Emagine continued to speak.

"She explained to you that not all stories have a happy ending. In her mind, the story of *Beauty and the Beast* ended the way it should have. Imagine what life would be like if there were no stories with happy endings. Mankind would fall into a state of hopelessness and despair."

"If what Nagama does here affects all of us, then how is it that I can still remember how things are supposed to be?"

"Good question," she replied with a smile. "As I mentioned a few moments ago, you are special, Alex. You, and a few others like you in your world, have a power that allows you to see beyond what is happening around you. You have the soul of a poet, the heart of a warrior, and the intelligence of a leader."

"So, why not just go in and undo what Nagama has done and restore the happy ending?"

"Another excellent question."

They stopped at one of the doors, and Lady Emagine tried to open it, but it was locked.

"Try to open this door," she said.

Alex stepped forward, reached out for the crystal doorknob, and tried the door for himself, but it would not budge.

"Behind this door lies the story of *Beauty and the Beast*. When Nagama entered this realm, he placed a magical spell on Beauty, and this caused her to never fall in love with Beast. She left him there alone in his castle and his love for her was so great that he died of a broken heart. Because the story is no longer a happy one, this doorway is now locked to us all. It will remain that way for all of eternity unless Nagama is defeated. Then, and only then, can the spell he placed on Beauty be broken and the story restored to the way it was written."

"How am I supposed to defeat a wizard like Nagama, if he is as powerful as you say? I am only a boy. I can't even handle the bullies that give me a hard time at my school."

"With this."

Lady Emagine raised her hands up and chanted softly as if she were casting a spell. She then brought them close to one another and cupped them together. A bright beautiful flash of light appeared for an instant and then vanished. As the light faded away, an object of some kind materialized in her hands. It was a necklace of some sort. She held it up to Alex.

"This is the Talisman of Harmony. It is a very ancient and very powerful talisman. Only someone who is pure of heart can wield it. As Nagama is a wizard with magical powers, you will need some magic of your own. The power contained within this Talisman can protect you, if and when you confront Nagama. It can be used to perform other magic, as well. When you need the power of the Talisman, simply clear your mind, concentrate on what you want to happen and say the words, *'Amor, et pacem'*, which, when translated, means *love, peace and happiness*. The Talisman's power will offer you protection, and it will carry out any command you give to it."

"*Amor, et pacem*," repeated Alex as he listened intently to Emagine's words.

She offered the Talisman to Alex. He reached up, took the necklace and put it around his neck. Then he tucked it inside of his tunic to conceal it from plain sight.

"I do not mean to rush things, but we mustn't waste any more time," cautioned Lady Emagine. "Nagama is already on the move, working to destroy another story's happy ending. You must now choose another door."

"How do I know which one to choose?" asked Alex.

"Do you remember when you first entered the hallway?"

Alex nodded and replied, "At first, I was a little bit afraid. The only thing I wanted to do was find my Mom. When I couldn't find her, I started to panic."

"But then reason took over, and you were able to calm yourself down," said Emagine. "You decided to open one of the doors to see if you could find her. How did you choose what door to open?"

"Well, once I calmed down, I got a funny feeling that sort of drew me to the door I went through."

"There is the answer to your question. You must calm yourself and clear your mind of everything else," she instructed. "Trust in your feelings. Allow your instincts to guide you to what you seek."

Alex closed his eyes and cleared his mind, as she had instructed. He let go of all the strange things that had happened to him thus far. He concentrated and then, after a moment, he opened his eyes. Alex began walking up and down the hallway. Then, as if by magic, an unseen force began drawing him further down the hallway, just as it had done when he first arrived here. Finally, he stopped in front one of the doors and looked up at it. He pointed to it, turned back towards Lady Emagine and smiled.

"Here," he said.

Emagine smiled and nodded at the youngster.

"Thank you, Lady Emagine. I will try my best to not let you and the Council down."

"I know you will, Alex. I have faith that you will have the strength and courage to face Nagama and put an end to his treachery, once and for all."

"See you soon," he said.

Alex reached out for the crystal-like doorknob, turned it and pulled. When the doorway swung open, he closed his eyes and stepped forward over the threshold. As it had happened before, the bright light appeared and disappeared.

Once on the other side of the doorway, Alex turned back, just in time to see it vanish, just as it had done when he went through the last one. He looked around at his new settings, and found himself in an open meadow. He looked down and noticed he was still dressed in the same clothes as he had worn in *Rumpelstiltskin*. He patted his tunic, where the Talisman was hidden. Confident that he had what he needed for his impending showdown with Nagama, he then set off on his quest to stop the evil wizard.

Nearby where he walked, there was a shallow stream. He strolled over to the bank of the stream, peered down into the water and noticed a school of striped fish swimming by. He then looked up and glanced off into the distance, where he saw a small village. There was a dirt road close by, cutting through the meadow which led up to the village, and so he decided to follow it.

When he arrived at the outskirts of the village, he hid behind one of the outer wooden shacks. He peered around the side of the building, looked around the village, trying to get his bearings and to determine which fairy tale he was in, now. Villagers walked about, carrying on with their daily life. Alex took notice that his clothing was much more sophisticated than the ones he saw the villagers wearing. He figured the clothes he was wearing, those of a nobleman, would make it rather difficult to anonymously blend into the crowd of villagers before him, so he ducked back behind the wooden shack and decided to give the Talisman a try.

He cleared his mind, just as Lady Emagine had taught him, and then he concentrated on his clothing. He trained his thoughts on changing the appearance of his clothes into something more common like the villagers wore. Then, he spoke out loud the magical words, "*Amor, et pacem.*" Instantly, his outfit was transformed from the noble attire he arrived in, into a common pair of trousers and a plain white shirt resembling the ones worn by the men and boys of the village.

Alex looked down at his clothing and smiled at himself for having done his first feat of magic. "Well, it worked," he congratulated himself. He then tucked the Talisman back into his shirt, hiding it from plain sight.

Alex stepped back out from behind the shack and began to explore the surrounding village. As he walked along the main street of the village, he happened past the opened window of a small house. He heard voices coming from inside. It was a woman talking to a boy.

"Oh Jack, my dear son. Our cow, Milky White, can no longer make milk for us to sell at the market. We have no money left to buy food. If we do not do something soon, we shall surely starve." She paused a moment, then continued, "I want you to take her to the market and sell her. Be sure that you get a fair price. Do not allow someone to trick you into selling her for far less than what she is worth."

"Oh, Mother, do we really have to sell Milky White? We have had her for years. She is my friend," said the boy disappointedly.

"I am sorry, my son. The money we had has run out, and we have nothing else of value to sell. We must sell her, if we are to eat."

"Yes, Mother," sadly replied the young boy.

As Alex listened in on the conversation, he realized this could only be Jack, from *Jack and the Beanstalk*, another favorite story of his. He watched as Jack came out of the house and went to the small pen standing next to the barn, where they kept their cow. Jack opened the stall and guided the animal out. He took a rope down from a hook on the pen's gate and tied it around the neck of the cow. Gently, he tugged on the rope.

"Come on girl," he said.

They began walking down the street towards the village market. Alex decided to follow behind them from a discreet distance hoping Jack would not notice.

The village's market place bustled with activity. There were villagers and merchants everywhere, haggling over prices, each trying to get the best deal they could. Jack walked around the market, talking to several of the merchants trying to get a fair offer for his cow. Few were interested, and those who were, did not want to give much for a cow who could no longer give milk. One man pointed across the market place and suggested that he try the butcher. Jack took Milky White over to the butcher's shop, where the butcher had a stand sitting outside his store. The butcher had a meat cleaver in his hand, and he was chopping up some sort of meat. When he saw Jack, he laid down the cleaver, wiped his hands on his apron and greeted the boy standing before him.

"Well, hello there, young lad," said the butcher as he extended his hand.

"Hello, sir," replied Jack, taking the butcher's hand and shaking it.

"Are you looking to sell that cow you have there?"

"Yes I am, sir. But I cannot seem to get a fair price for her. Nobody here seems to be interested in buying a cow that can no longer give milk."

"Let me see what you have here," he replied.

The butcher stepped away from his stand and walked to the side of the cow. He took a few moments to look Milky White over. He rubbed the side of the animal and checked to see that the cow was healthy. Then, he finally turned back to Jack and said, "Well, my young lad, it is lucky for you that you ran into me. I'll tell you what I am going to do. I recently came across these..."

He reached into the pocket of his apron. When he pulled his hand out, he turned it upright, and opened it. In his hand were what appeared to be five ordinary looking beans. He moved them around in his hand as he showed them to Jack.

Jack looked at the beans carefully then considered the man standing before him. He was a tall yet plump man. He had a clean shaven head, thick bushy eyebrows and a mustache long enough to cover his upper lip. He gave the butcher a strange and suspicious look.

"Those are not money" he said. "They are common, everyday beans. Not even enough for a meal. Are you trying to trick me?" he asked.

"No, my boy. These beans may look ordinary, but these have been imbued with magical powers."

Jack's ears perked up. "Magic you say?"

The butcher closed the hand with the beans and placed it over his heart, while he raised the other in the air, as if attesting to authenticity of his claim. "Yes. I swear on me Mother's grave. If you plant them tonight, by morning they will grow into a stalk so grand that it will reach up to the sky."

Jack thought it over for a moment. He knew that magical beans would be a much better deal than any of the other offers he had received today.

"Very well, sir," he said. "You have bought yourself a cow."

"Excellent, here you are, me boy" replied the butcher as he offered the beans to Jack.

Jack took the five magical beans from the man, put them in his pocket, and in turn, he handed the rope tied around Milky White's neck to the butcher. He walked over to the side of his longtime companion, gave her one last rub down, and said a quiet, sad goodbye. Then he turned slowly and began his walk back home. Alex followed Jack back to his house, keeping his distance as they walked along.

When Jack arrived at his home, he was very excited about his trade with the butcher, and he immediately showed his mother the magical beans. He was proud that he got such a great deal for Milky White; his mother, not so much. Alex listened outside the window. He could hear that Jack's mother was very angry with him.

"Beans! You traded Milky White for five common beans?" she yelled in frustration. "What were you thinking, son?"

"But Mother, these beans are magical" he said, trying to defend his decision. "The butcher told me that if we plant them tonight, they will grow into a stalk that will reach up to the sky by morning."

"Magical! Magical?" she countered. "There is no such thing as magic, my misguided son. I am so disappointed in you, Jack."

Jack's mother took the beans from him, walked to the window and threw open the curtains.

Fearing that he might be discovered, Alex ducked in behind a nearby bush in order to remain hidden. Jack's mother stuck her hand outside of the window and dropped the beans on to the ground below.

"But Mother," protested Jack.

"Enough talk about magical beans!" she said, anger still in her voice. "You will go to bed this minute, and you will do it without any supper. In the meantime, I have to figure out what we are going to do now that we have nothing left."

Jack hung his head low and did as his mother told him. He climbed up the steps that led to his room. From the top of the stairs, he could hear his mother crying. He felt really bad about making her cry.

He called out to her from upstairs, "Mother, I am sorry I let you down."

"Just go to bed, son," came the response from below.

Sadly, Jack turned towards his room, went inside and closed the door.

Outside, Alex began to look around for a place where he might spend the night. He went to Jack's barn, and once inside, he spotted several bales of hay. He stacked the bales up in such a way that he could stay out of sight, but still keep watch over Jack's house.

Soon, the sun went down, and the village began to settle in for the evening. The night air carried a chill. From his hiding place, Alex shivered. He was tired from his long day, but he fought to stay awake. Several times, he started to nod off to sleep.

Suddenly, there was a strange noise coming from outside the barn. It sounded like dry twigs being stepped on. Alex knew the snapping sound of the twigs signaled that someone was approaching the house. Carefully and quietly, he peered out from his hiding place, to see if he could spot the intruder.

A dark figure, dressed all in black, walked past his hiding place. The cloaked man did not notice Alex, as he walked over to the window where the beans had landed when Jack's mom threw them out. The stranger bent over, gathered up the beans and rolled them around in his hand for a moment. Then, he put them into a coin purse and hooked it onto his belt. The dark figure turned back towards the direction from which he had come and began to walk away from the small house.

"That must have been Nagama," Alex commented to himself.

He realized that he had to act fast so he considered what his options were and what he could do to get the magical beans back where they belonged. He knew that without the beans, the beanstalk would not grow. And if it did not grow, then the adventure would end here, before it even got started, and there would be no happy ending for Jack and his mother. It was likely they would end up homeless and be forced to wander the streets of their village, begging for scraps. The thought of that ending did not set well with Alex.

He decided he had to take action now and find some means to get the beans back, so he set off to follow the stranger. He trailed the dark figure, staying hidden in the shadows, much like he and Lord Deker had done when they approached the little man's camp in the last story he visited. He looked for an opportunity to present itself for him to take back the magical beans.

As the dark figure neared a neighbor's barn, Alex crept around to the other side of the building. He tried to think of some kind of ploy that would allow him to take the beans from Nagama, so that he could put them back in their place outside Jack's window.

"Think, Alex," he quietly said to himself.

He glanced around the area for a moment, looking for some means of getting the coin purse away from the dark wizard. He spotted a stick lying on the ground nearby and picked it up. He studied it more closely. The end of the stick was shaped like a hook. If he could distract the evil wizard for a moment and catch the coin purse at the right angle, then maybe he could use this stick to take back the magical beans.

He moved to the far side of the barn and hid in the darkness. He pulled out the Talisman and cleared his mind. When Nagama passed by the barn, Alex whispered the magical words, *"Amor, et pacem,"* as he called upon the power of the Talisman.

Suddenly there was a faint noise that caused Nagama to stop and look around. Alex quickly and gently snagged the coin purse with the stick he had found. The dark wizard seemed unaware that his coin purse had been taken. When Nagama was sure no one was there, he continued on his journey and left the village.

Once the black-cloaked wizard was out of sight, Alex sprang from his hiding spot, and he ran all the way back to Jack's house. There, he put the beans back where they belonged, just outside the window of Jack's house.

Feeling like he had completed his mission, Alex looked around, expecting the door to reappear, but it did not. Finally after several moments of waiting, he determined that his work here was not yet completed, so he returned to his hiding place in the barn and kept watch on the house for the rest of the night.

Throughout the night and into the dawn, the beanstalk grew. By morning, it reached all the way up to the sky, just as the butcher had promised. Alex sat and stared in awe at the mighty beanstalk.

From the second floor of the small house, where Jack's room was, Alex saw the young boy look out of his window at the giant beanstalk. Jack, who was still wearing his night shirt, looked upwards following the beanstalk with his eyes, and he saw that it disappeared up into the clouds.

He ducked back into his room for a few moments, and when he came back to the window, Alex could see that he had changed out of the nightshirt and was now dressed in a shirt and pair of pants.

Jack climbed out of his window and scurried up the beanstalk. Alex watched Jack as he climbed high up the beanstalk, and soon, he disappeared into the clouds. Alex moved from Jack's barn to the streets of the village, so he could keep a better watch on the beanstalk. He decided, for now, he should sit and wait for Jack to return, so he took a seat on a bench across from Jack's house.

The people of the village passed by Alex, while he waited for Jack to come down the beanstalk. Most were heading off to begin their day at work. Nobody seemed to take notice of the giant beanstalk growing next to Jack's house. This amused Alex. "How can they not see that thing? It's huge!"

A few of the passing villagers nodded to Alex or bid him a good day. Alex smiled and returned their greetings.

After a couple of hours went by, Alex spotted Jack climbing back down the beanstalk from the clouds. He seemed to be carrying something with him. Alex took a moment to recall the last time his mother, Sarah, read the story to him. Soon, he realized that Jack had to be carrying the two bags of gold he had taken from the Giant's home in the clouds.

When Jack reached the bottom of the beanstalk, he climbed back into his window and went down the stairs. Alex moved in closer to the small house, so he could better hear what was happening. He heard Jack and his mom talking. She sounded overjoyed and filled with excitement.

"Oh, my good son," she said. "What is this you bring to us?"

"It is gold, Mother, two bags full of gold," he replied.

"I do not know why I ever doubted you, my sweet boy. There is enough gold here, so that we may live well for quite some time. From where did you get this, my son?" she asked.

Jack paused for a moment to think, about how he should answer his mother's question. He did not want to lie to her, but he also did not want to give her cause to worry about him. Finally, after a long moment he told her, "This gold comes to us, because I sold Milky White to the butcher for five magical beans, yesterday. Now, I know that you do not believe in magic, Mother, but here is the proof they are what I said they were. I had a feeling, when I made that deal with the butcher, that there was indeed magic in those beans."

"I am sorry for getting so angry with you yesterday and for doubting you. I will never doubt you again, my son. Now run along and play with your friends."

Alex moved away from the window and returned to his hiding spot. A moment later, he saw Jack run outside his door. Jack looked around for his friends, but he did not see any of them about. He went over to a tree near the barn and began climbing it. When he got up high enough, he could see Alex, hiding in the barn, behind the stacked bales of hay.

"Hello there," said Jack, as he hung upside down from a tree branch.

"Hi. How are you?"

"I am Jack. What are you doing hiding in our hay bales?"

"My name is Alex. I was pretending that a mean ogre was after me, and I had to find a place to hide, or he would get me and eat me up. So, I stacked the bales of hay up like they were the walls of a castle, so he would not find me. I did not think anyone would mind. I am sorry if I did something wrong."

"You did nothing wrong. I am pleased to meet you, Alex. Would you like to play with me?"

"Yes, I would," replied Alex. "That sounds like a lot of fun."

Jack climbed down from the tree. He walked over to where Alex stood and shook hands with him. Then he tagged Alex on the shoulder, and began to run away. He yelled out over his shoulder, "Tag, you're it!"

Alex gave chase after Jack, and the two boys ran throughout the village, tagging one another. With each tag, the direction of the chase changed. During one of the rounds, Jack had a considerable lead on Alex, and he had run behind a rickety old building. He hid behind some barrels that were stacked there and watched as Alex ran by. From his hiding place, he laughed as Alex stopped to look around, searching for his new friend.

"Jack?" he called out. "Where did you go?"

"I am hiding. Come and find me."

Alex followed the sound of Jack's voice to the building where the barrels were stacked up against the outside wall. He slowly snuck around to the one side of the barrels, but Jack was not there. Jack had crept around to the other side, opposite of his hiding spot, when Alex came to search behind the barrels. Alex knew Jack was somewhere nearby, so he switched his direction and went back the way he came. Once on the other side, he found Jack sitting there, laughing.

"There you are," said Alex, joining in the laughter.

"Your turn to hide. I will count to twenty."

Alex looked around the village for a moment, trying to find a good hiding spot. When he found one, he looked around for just a bit longer, so his eyes would not give away his choice. He turned back to Jack and said, "Okay. Go!"

Jack turned back towards the barrels and hid his face. He began counting.

"One. Two. Three..."

Alex scurried off to his hiding place. He decided to hide in the nearby village stables. There was a loft above it, and he was sure he could find a good place to hide there. He dashed into the stables and climbed up the rickety ladder leading into the hay loft. The rungs of the ladder made a creaking noise as he climbed up towards the loft.

As Alex reached the top of the ladder, he saw a large heap of hay piled up in the corner. He hurried over to the hay stack and began covering himself up to make it harder for Jack to find him. He could hear Jack finishing up his count.

"Eighteen. Nineteen. Twenty. Ready or not, you shall be caught, here I come!"

Jack uncovered his eyes and looked around the area for any signs of where Alex might be hiding. He jogged around the village square area looking in and around any of the many possible hiding places. Alex was nowhere to be found. He walked into a few of the local shops to see if his new friend had ducked inside one of them to hide.

Still nothing. He returned back to the center of the square, near where the stables were and looked around the area once again.

"You are very good at hide and seek, Alex," he called out.

Just then, he heard a faint snicker coming from off in the distance, where the horse stables were. It sounded as if someone were laughing, but trying very hard not to make a sound. Jack started to walk towards the building. When he reached the door, he popped his head in to see if anyone was there. When he saw nobody, he quietly walked in. As he crossed the threshold of the door, he noticed a few pieces of hay falling through the slats from the hay loft above. He went to the ladder and climbed it as slowly and quietly as he could or rather as quietly as the creaking rungs would allow.

When he reached the top, he looked around for Alex. He knew his friend had to be somewhere up here in the loft. He noticed the pile of hay sitting in the corner of the loft. He studied it closely for a moment. Then, suddenly, it moved. Jack quietly inched forward. When he stood over the pile of hay, he yelled out and grabbed at the hay. Alex let out a loud burst of laughter, and gathered up a hand full of hay and tossed it at Jack. Jack returned the playful gesture. Both boys fell back onto the soft hay and continued laughing.

It took several minutes for them both to settle down. Jack looked at Alex and said, "I am glad that I met you, Alex. You are so fun to play with."

"I feel the same way, too, Jack. I haven't had this much fun in a long time. I don't have too many friends at home."

"Well, you have one here." Jack smiled and paused a moment then said, "Hey! There is a pond nearby, just over the hill, and it has a dock. We can go there and see if we can spot any fish swimming around."

"Okay. That sounds like fun."

So the boys decided to take a break from the games. They used the ladder to climb down from the hay loft and walked outside. Jack pointed off into the distance and said, "The pond is this way, just over the rise of that hill, there."

Alex followed Jack. It took several minutes for the boys to walk the distance from the village to the pond.

When the boys arrived at the pond, they headed straight for the dock that was built on the shoreline. They leaned over the side and peered into the crystal clear waters below. Schools of varying fish were swimming all around the dock area.

"Wow! Look at all of those fish. They are everywhere!" exclaimed Alex.

"Yes, and look at the big one, there," replied Jack as he pointed to a catfish swimming near the dock.

"Oh my goodness! He is huge! My uncle would love to catch one that size."

"Your uncle is a fisherman?" asked Jack.

"Not really. He works as a carpenter, but he loves to go fishing, whenever he is not busy with his work. My aunt goes with him on his fishing trips, but she does not like to fish. She usually just reads a book, while he fishes. Sometimes though, he takes me with him, too."

"When you went with him, did you ever skip rocks on the water?"

"Yes, once he and I went on an overnight fishing trip. We set up camp near a river and that evening, we walked along the shore, picking up rocks and sailing them across the water."

Jack walked back to the shore of the pond. There, he gathered up several rocks of different shape and size. He brought them back to the end of the dock and set them all down on the ground, except for one.

"Watch this."

Jack looked out across the pond to make sure nobody was in that direction, then with a side cast from his arm, he threw the stone. When it hit the water, it skipped along and Jack counted the skips aloud.

"One. Two. Three. Four. Five."

After five skips, the stone's momentum finally slowed enough that it sank into the water below. Ripples of water showed the path in which the stone had traveled before it finally went under. Moments later, the ripples dissipated, and the pond was calm once again.

"Wow!" said Alex. "Five skips. That was pretty good. Let's see if I can match it."

Alex carefully looked over the pile of rocks and finally made a choice. He chose the flattest rock he could find. Like Jack, he too looked out across the pond to make sure there was nobody in the direction he was going to throw. When he was sure the coast was clear, he let loose the stone. It skipped along the water, much like the way Jack's stone had. The boys counted aloud together, "One. Two. Three. Four." Then the rock stopped and sank.

"Oh!" said Alex with mock disappointment. "Almost tied you."

"Yes. I thought for sure it had another skip left in it."

Jack picked up another stone and sent it sailing across the pond. Then Alex took his turn. They continued on, counting aloud the skips, until there were no more stones to throw.

Then, Jack sat down on the edge of the dock and removed his shoes. He put the shoes aside and then dangled his feet into the water, scaring the fish away for the time being. Alex sat beside him, took off his own shoes and did the same.

"So Alex, where do you come from?"

"I am from a village far, far away. My mother is visiting friends nearby, and I was out to play when you first saw me."

"What about your father?"

"My father got very sick a few years ago. There was nothing that could be done to help him get better, so he went to be with God in Heaven."

"Ah," nodded Jack. "You and I have something in common, then. I too lost my father, when I was but a baby. I, very much, miss not getting to know him. My mother still talks of him to this day. She often tells me what a good, kind and brave man he was."

"I miss my father, too. I was lucky enough to know him before he left. Like your father, he was a good man. Every night before I went to bed, he and my mother would tell me stories of adventure or honor or just something funny."

"Adventure? You like stories of adventure?"

Alex nodded.

"Well, I had an adventure earlier today. Can you guess what I did?

"No. What did you do?"

Jack smiled at Alex and began to recount the events of his journey to the clouds earlier that morning.

"To tell it in full, I must start with what happened yesterday."

"We, my mother and I, are by no means a rich family. In fact, we had no money left to buy food. My mother had asked me to take our cow, Milky White, to the village square market area and sell her because the cow was the only thing left of value that we owned. I did as I was told and took Milky White to the market place. I could not find anyone willing to give me a fair price. One man suggested I try the butcher's shop. The butcher was unwilling to spend much money on a cow that could no longer produce milk, so he offered me five magical beans, instead. I thought to myself, magical beans seemed like a fair trade. I agreed and went home to tell mother about my trade. She did not believe me, when I told her the beans were magical, and she got very angry with me. She threw the beans out of the window and sent me to bed without any supper."

"When I awoke this morning, my room was very dark. I jumped out of my bed and went to the window to find out why no light shined in. The sun was out and shining brightly, but from the ground beside my window, there was this enormous and great beanstalk. It stretched up and up into the sky, up as far as my eyes could see. Up into the clouds. I said to myself, 'I'll just see where this beanstalk leads.'"

"I change out of my nightshirt, stepped out of my window onto the beanstalk and began to climb upwards. Several minutes of climbing went by, and I looked down. I saw my house and from where I was; it was a mere speck below. I looked back up towards the heavens and continued my climb, until I finally reached the top."

"At the top of the beanstalk, I found myself in a new and wondrous land with a beautiful countryside. Far off in the distance, there was a great and mighty castle. Next to where the beanstalk came through the clouds was a long and enormous cobblestoned road leading up to the gate of the grand castle. I began to walk along the road towards the gate. Along the way, I was surprised to meet a beautiful maiden who had suddenly appeared beside me."

"'Good Morning, Miss,' I said."

"'Good morning, Jack,' she replied."

"I was surprised; she knew my name, so I asked her, 'How do you know who I am?'"

"'I know much more than just your name, Jack,' she replied, 'For instance, I know that you are the son of a brave and gallant knight, who once fought to protect the people of your village, but he was slain by the foul giant who lives in that castle you see over there. This happened long ago when you were just a baby. When your father fell to the giant, your mother vowed never to tell you this, in the hopes of sparing you the pain. She did not want you to grow up feeling the need to exact revenge. All that the giant owns, now belongs to you and your mother.'"

"The maiden suddenly disappeared in a flash of light, and I thought to myself, 'I bet she was an angel, or at the very least, a fairy.'"

"I continued to walk down the long road towards the castle. When I arrived at the gate, I saw the Giant's wife standing at the huge doorway. She was sweeping with a broom that was bigger than my house. I walked up to her and said, 'Excuse me, ma'am, could you find it in your heart to give me some breakfast? I have had nothing to eat since yesterday's lunch.'"

"The Giant's wife turned to see who was talking to her. She looked around and then looked downwards at me. Though she was very big and very ugly, she did have a kind heart. She smiled at me."

"'Very well, young man,' she said, leaning the massive broom against the wall, "you may come into the castle, but we must be quick about it. If my husband, the Giant, finds out you are here, he will grind you up and make bread of you. Then, he will gobble you up, bones and all.'"

"I followed the Giant's wife into the castle. She led me to the kitchen, and there, she gave me breakfast. While I was eating though, there came a loud knock at the castle door that shook the walls."

"'Who can that be?' I asked."

"'Oh my! That is my husband, the Giant. Quick! We must hide you.'"

"The Giant's wife looked around the kitchen for a place to hide me, then she lifted me up and placed me into the empty cold oven. Next, she went to the door, opened it up and let her husband in. The Giant walked through the doorway, stopped, and sniffed at the air."

"With a loud and enormous voice, he yelled, *'Fee, fi, fo, fum. I smell the blood of an Englishman. Be he alive, or be he dead, I'll grind his bones to make my bread!'*"

"The Giant's wife rolled her eyes and looked around the room, and not seeing any Englishman there, she replied, 'That is utter nonsense, you must be mistaken. It is your breakfast you smell. Now sit down and I will get you your food.'"

"The Giant looked around as well. Like his wife, he did not see any Englishman about, so he took his wife at her word and sat down to eat his breakfast. After he finished his food, he looked up at his wife, who was washing the dishes, and said, 'Woman, bring me my money.'"

"His wife dried off her hands. She went to the cabinet in The Giant's counting room and brought him two bags full of gold. He began to count his money. As he counted, he soon began to yawn. It seemed, as if, he could hardly keep his eyes open. He closed his eyes and a few moments later, he was fast asleep. Soon after, the Giant began to snore a loud and thunderous snore. I decided to wait a little longer in my hiding place, just to be sure."

"When I was sure he was asleep, I snuck out from my sanctuary in the oven. Sure enough, The Giant was there in his chair, fast asleep. Let me tell you, friend, he was a huge and vile looking creature, with an ogre-like face, and skin as pale as snow. He was dank with sweat, causing an odor so foul, that it smelled of death. At his side, was the gold I had heard him counting. I snatched up the bags of gold and ran for the door. I left the castle far behind and ran all the way back to the beanstalk, where I climbed it back down to the safety of my own room. I took the two bags of gold downstairs to where my mother was and showed them to her. She was so surprised at the sight of the gold, and it made her happy that we now had enough money to live on."

"Wow! You really had an adventure."

"Yes, that I did!"

Jack looked up at the sky. It was late in the afternoon, and the sun was beginning to set for the evening.

"It is starting to get late. I must go home now. Mother will have supper ready soon. I am glad to have met you, Alex. Maybe I will see you again, tomorrow."

"I hope so, Jack; I had a lot of fun playing with you, today."

The two boys put their shoes back on, stood up, and shook hands. Jack turned away from the dock and began walking towards his house. He turned back to look at Alex once more and waved goodbye, then he disappeared over the rise of the hill. Alex waited a little longer, allowing Jack to get a good head start before he followed.

Alex hurried back to his hiding place in Jack's barn, so that he could watch over Jack's house. The sun went down and before long, the moon rose up into the night sky. Like the night before, there was a bit of a chill in the air. Alex had found a blanket that was once used to cover Milky White on cold nights. He took the blanket to his hiding spot and used it to stay warm.

Soon the lights from the village went out one by one, until there were none. The village was asleep.

Alex was tired from his long day of play with Jack, and he was finding it hard to stay awake. The night was eerily quiet. Without meaning to, he closed his eyes and fell asleep amongst the hay bales.

Suddenly a flash of smoke appeared and a dark figure materialized out of thin air, next to the beanstalk.

It was Nagama again, dressed head to toe in his black cloak. He looked up skyward, where the beanstalk entered the clouds. He cast a spell that began lifting him in midair. The power of the spell allowed him to rise up alongside the great beanstalk, and soon, he disappeared into the clouds.

Once on the other side of the clouds, like Jack before him, the evil Nagama traveled along the broad cobblestoned road up to the castle gate. He used his magical powers to unlock and push open the enormous castle door. Silently, he moved inside.

In the distance, he could hear the Giant snoring loudly. He followed the sound to the bedroom, and there he found The Giant and his wife fast asleep in their bed.

"What a vile set of creatures, and that smell," he whispered. "Yet, one has a good heart. I will have to do something to change that."

Nagama took out his wand and quietly chanted as he began casting a spell. He focused his spell on the Giant's sleeping wife.

"For all the kindness you may know, it is the time for it to go. When someone needs your help this day, the goodness in you goes away."

A spark of reddish-orange light shot out from the tip of Nagama's wand and struck the Giant's wife. She shifted in her bed, but not enough to stir her from her sleep.

"Let us see how that troublesome Jack fares the next time he visits here," Nagama laughed quietly.

He turned around to leave The Giant's bedroom as quietly as he came, and then he made his way back to the opened front door.

Once outside, he used his magic to close the massive door and lock it. Nagama left the castle and walked back to the beanstalk. There, he again cast his magic levitation spell and flew back to the ground below. As he touched down, he waved his wand again, and he disappeared in a puff of black billowy smoke.

Something stirred Alex from his sleep, a strange noise had awakened him from his slumber. He looked around and saw that nothing seemed amiss. He shook his head to clear the cobwebs from his mind.

"Whoa! Got to try to stay awake," Alex said as he rubbed the sleep from his eyes and went back to his vigil of watching over Jack's house.

Hours had passed, and Alex yawned, as the sun rose. It had been a very long night. Though he was tired, he was just as determined in his quest to stop Nagama's evil plans.

The village was slowly waking from its sleep, and soon there was a bustle of activity throughout the market square. Merchants were opening up their stands, ready to begin another day of trading. Children were running about, playing in the streets, while their parents left home and started their day of work.

Alex turned and looked back towards Jack's house. The front door opened, and Jack's mother came outside. She was carrying an empty basket. She closed the front door behind her and headed off in the direction of the square to do some shopping.

Alex stood up and began folding the blanket he had used to stay warm. He went into the barn to put it away. When he returned to his observation post, a small commotion near Jack's bedroom window caught his eye. He studied the window a bit closer and saw the leaves from the beanstalk rustling about. A moment later, he saw Jack come out of the window and grab hold of the branches on the mighty beanstalk. When he was securely in place, Jack once again climbed skyward and began his ascent up towards the clouds.

Alex sat in his hiding place and watched over the area, while he waited for Jack to come back down. An hour later he noticed Jack's mom returning to her home from her shopping spree at the marketplace. She had her basket with her, and it now was full of food. Alex noticed something else. She was pulling a rope and tied to the other end of it was none other than Milky White, Jack's cow.

"She must have gone to see the butcher and bought the cow back. Jack will be so happy to have his friend back," Alex thought to himself.

Jack's mother brought the cow to the pen and put Milky White back into her stall. She coiled up the rope and put it back onto the hook on the pen's gate. She rubbed the cow's side, smiled and went back into the house. To Alex, the cow seemed almost relieved to be back in familiar surroundings.

As more time had passed and Jack had not come back down the beanstalk, Alex started to get worried. If all was going as he remembered, Jack should have been back by now, carrying the goose that lays golden eggs.

"I hope he is Okay."

A few minutes more and Alex could not wait any longer. Something had to have gone wrong, he determined.

From the hiding place, he checked around the area to see if the coast was clear. Once he was certain he would not be seen by any of the villagers, he sprinted towards the beanstalk and began climbing it himself.

Halfway up the beanstalk, he looked down at the ground below. The people were moving around the village like a colony of little ants. He turned his attention back to the beanstalk and continued his own ascent.

When he finally reached the top of the beanstalk, he saw what Jack had described to him in his adventure. The Giant's castle was off in the distance, and it had a long and broad cobblestoned road leading up to it. Alex ran the distance of the broad road. He had to get to the castle, fast. He was worried for his friend.

As he neared the castle, he slowed down and moved more cautiously and quietly. He snuck up to the gargantuan-sized castle door which was slightly ajar, and with one more check of his surroundings, he squeezed through the opening and went inside.

When he entered the castle, he was startled by a sudden glimpse of The Giant. He calmed himself, when he realized The Giant was in his chair, fast asleep.

Just as Jack had described, The Giant was gruesomely ugly. However, Jack's description of the stench coming from the giant paled in comparison to his actually smelling it. This was a smell that was worse than death, and it would be an odor that Alex would not soon forget.

He looked around the room for any sign of Jack. There was a large table sitting on the other side of the room, and on it was a bird cage. In comparison to himself, the bird cage was huge, as large as his bedroom at home.

Alex took a closer look at the cage and saw that Jack was locked up inside. Jack appeared to be looking for a means to escape from his prison.

Alex quietly ran across the room, over to the table and took cover behind one of its legs. When he was sure the coast was clear, he began to climb up the leg. As he reached the top of the table, he peered over the edge. There he saw The Giant's steel drinking cup. It would be big enough for him to hide behind so he climbed onto the table top and ran to it. He looked towards the bird cage and waved his hands wildly in the air, trying to draw Jack's attention, but Jack did not notice him there.

Alex looked around for something he could use to get Jack's attention, but he could only find crumbs left over from The Giant's lunch. He picked up one of the crumbs that was about the size of a small stone. He looked at it a moment, shrugged, then tossed it towards the cage. The crumb hit the side of the cage without making much noise, but it was a loud enough sound to get Jack's attention. Jack started looking around the room to see where the crumb came from. Finally, he saw Alex hiding behind the enormous cup.

Jack looked towards The Giant to see that he was still asleep and then looked about the massive room to see that The Giant's wife was nowhere near. When he was sure the wife was not around, he motioned to Alex that it was safe to move. Alex quietly crept across the table and up to the side of the cage opposite to where The Giant slept.

Jack breathed a sigh of relief and whispered, "I really thought I was to meet my maker, or at the very least, be an ingredient in The Giant's next meal."

"What happened?" asked Alex.

"I climbed up the beanstalk, just as I did yesterday. When I got here to the castle, I saw the Giant's wife. She offered to make me another breakfast. I was hungry so I said 'yes'. When the Giant came home she told me to hide again, but this time, when he walked into the castle, she led him straight to the cold oven and showed him where I was hiding."

Alex looked around the table top for something with which he could use to pry the cage door open. The eating utensils were too large for Alex to use, not to mention dangerously close to the sleeping Giant's hand.

A little further away from The Giant, there was his wife's sewing basket sitting near the edge of the table. Alex could see that inside the basket was a spool of thread with a needle wedged in it.

Alex crept over to the basket and climbed in. He crawled over to the spool and began working the needle free from it. When he finally got it loose from the spool, he climbed back out of the sewing basket, checked to see that The Giant was still sleeping, then he went back to Jack and the cage. Alex used the tip of the needle to pick the lock on the cage. The door finally unlocked with a faint click. Alex carefully pulled on the cage door, trying not to make any unnecessary noise. When the door opened, Jack stepped out onto the table top.

"Quick!" Alex said cautiously and quietly. "We have to get out of here before The Giant wakes up from his nap."

Jack started to leave with Alex, but then he hesitated for a moment.

"Wait," he whispered.

"What's wrong?" asked Alex.

"The Giant keeps a goose that lays golden eggs, and he also has a harp that can play the most beautiful of melodies. We should get them before we leave."

"Where does he keep them?"

"There." Jack pointed to where The Giant kept the goose. "And there," he said, pointing at the harp on a nearby shelf.

"We have to hurry before something or someone wakes him up, and we end up staying as his dinner." Alex paused a moment then said, "Okay. You get the harp, and I will go for the goose."

Jack headed for the enchanted harp, and Alex made his way towards the magical goose. They grabbed them up at the same time, but as Jack tucked the harp under his arm, its strings made a noise. The Giant stirred and woke up. He rubbed the sleep from his eyes and shook the cobwebs from his head. Then, noticed the two boys trying to take away his prized possessions. He became angry and began to growl.

"Fee, fi, fo, fum. I smell the blood of two Englishmen. Be they alive, or be they dead, I'll grind their bones to make my bread!"

"Run!" yelled Alex.

The two boys scampered from the room and ran towards the door of the castle.

The Giant stood up from his chair, where he had fallen asleep and went to the corner of his counting room. There he grabbed a huge wooden club and gave chase after Alex and Jack.

The boys squeezed through the opening in the castle door and ran away from the castle as fast as they could. They headed down the broad cobblestoned road, towards the beanstalk.

The Giant was in hot pursuit, carrying his large wooden club. The ground shook with each of his footsteps. He caught up to the fleeing boys and swung the club at Jack, barely missing him. He swung again at Alex but missed him by a mile. The boys ran through small cracks and brush trying to evade The Giant.

Then, The Giant suddenly stumbled and fell to the ground with a thunderous crash. This gave the boys a chance to gain a longer lead on The Giant, who was picking himself up off of the ground. They made it all the way back to the beanstalk, but The Giant was only moments behind. Together, they climbed downward towards the village below.

The Giant slowed up when he reached the beanstalk. He looked down towards the ground, searching for his prey. When he spotted the boys, he roared out loud, "You shall not get away this time!" He grabbed ahold of the mighty beanstalk and followed Jack and Alex down towards the village below.

The two boys climbed downwards as fast as they could. The tiny village grew bigger and bigger, as they got closer to the earth. Jack spotted his mother who was tending to her garden. When they were close enough, Jack yelled down to her.

"Mother! Get the axe from the barn! Mother!"

Jack's Mother looked up from her garden and glanced around the garden. She could have sworn she just heard her son.

"Mother!"

Jack's Mother looked up towards the beanstalk and saw Jack and another boy climbing down. She looked further up and saw the Giant who had slain her husband, chasing after her son. Her worst fear was coming to pass. She was suddenly very angry and very frightened.

"Oh my dear Lord! My son!"

"Mother! Bring me the axe from the barn."

Jack's Mother put down her gardening tool and ran to the barn. There, she fetched the axe that was hanging on the wall, and then ran back to the beanstalk.

Jack and Alex reach the ground just as she got back. Jack set the harp down and took the axe from his mother. He began chopping at the beanstalk.

The Giant was determined not to lose his prey, and he continued climbing downwards.

Jack chopped as fast as he could. The beanstalk started to make crackling noises as the fibers in the stalk began to snap from the cutting. Jack gave it another few chops, then he dropped the axe on the ground. He began pushing against the beanstalk with all his might. Alex put down the goose and started pushing as well. The mighty beanstalk continued to crackle and splinter. Jack's mother joined in the effort to push on the beanstalk. Then, it began to fall. Slowly at first, then faster as gravity took over.

"Timber!" yelled Alex.

The Giant tried desperately to hold on, but he lost his grip on the beanstalk and began falling towards the ground below. He hit the earth with a deafening crash, creating a large crater where he landed. The beanstalk fell into the crater on top of him, creating a cloud of dust and debris, which rose up from the massive hole in the ground. The Giant was no more.

Alex raised his arms up in triumph. "Yes! We did it!" The boys congratulated one another as they celebrated their victory over The Giant.

Jack's Mother wrapped her arms around her son thankful that he was alright.

Jack pulled back from his Mother and turned his head towards Alex. "Mother. I would like for you to meet my friend, Alex. He saved me from The Giant, when I was captured."

She smiled at Alex and said, "I am pleased to meet you, Alex. Thank you for saving my son."

"It was nothing, Ma'am."

"Nothing you say?" replied Jack with a surprised look on his face. "You risked everything for me, and you helped me to avenge my father's death. I can never repay the debt I owe you."

"That is what friends do for one another. Through thick or thin they are always at your side, ready to back you up."

Suddenly, there was a shimmering light, and the door leading back to the hallway appeared behind Alex. He did not notice it at first but when Jack's eyes grew wide open with disbelief, he turned around to look.

"What it that?" asked a bewildered Jack.

"That is where I came from and where I must go back to, now."

"But, Alex, I do not want you to leave."

"I know how you feel, but I have to go back."

Alex extended his hand to Jack who took it. The two boys shook and said their farewells.

"Fear not my friend," said Alex with a smile, "We will see one another again, someday."

Then unexpectedly, there came a sound from the pen next to the barn. It was the sound of a cow. Jack looked towards the pen and then to his mother. She smiled and nodded.

"I went to visit the butcher at the market today and bought Milky White back from him. I know how much you love her. Now that we have the money, I could just not leave her there." Jack wrapped his arms around his mother's waist, giving her a hug.

"Thank you, mother."

Alex smiled at both mother and son. He turned towards the door. Before walking through, he looked back at Jack and his mom, one last time, as they both walked back into their little cottage. Jack turned and waved at Alex, who waved back, then Alex turned back to the door and walked through.

Alex reentered the Hall of a Thousand Doors where he found Lady Emagine waiting there for him. She had a profound look of uneasiness on her face.

"Are you alright, Alex?"

"Yes, I am fine, My Lady. Thank you for your concern. That was awful close there when The Giant came after us. Lucky for us he tripped and fell. That gave us just enough time to get away."

"Yes it was close. Too close. You must be more careful. I can do nothing to protect you, when you are inside one of the doors."

"I understand," replied Alex.

"You did a fine job stopping Nagama and helping Jack's story conclude with a happy ending. I knew I was right about you."

"It was fun to actually to play a role in the story. Before, when my Mom read to me, I could only use my imagination to feel like I was a part of the story. This way is so much better."

"Well your work is not yet complete. You will need to hurry before Nagama strikes again and tries to destroy another happy ending. It is time to choose another door."

Alex began to walk up and down the hallway trying to pick the next door he would go through. As he passed by one of the doors, he got that same strange feeling. Like before, he stopped, pointed to a door, and turned to Lady Emagine.

"This one," he said.

Lady Emagine nodded.

"Please be careful, Alex. Do not take any unnecessary risks."

"I won't, My Lady. I will see you, when I return."

Alex turned back to the door, opened it and walked through.

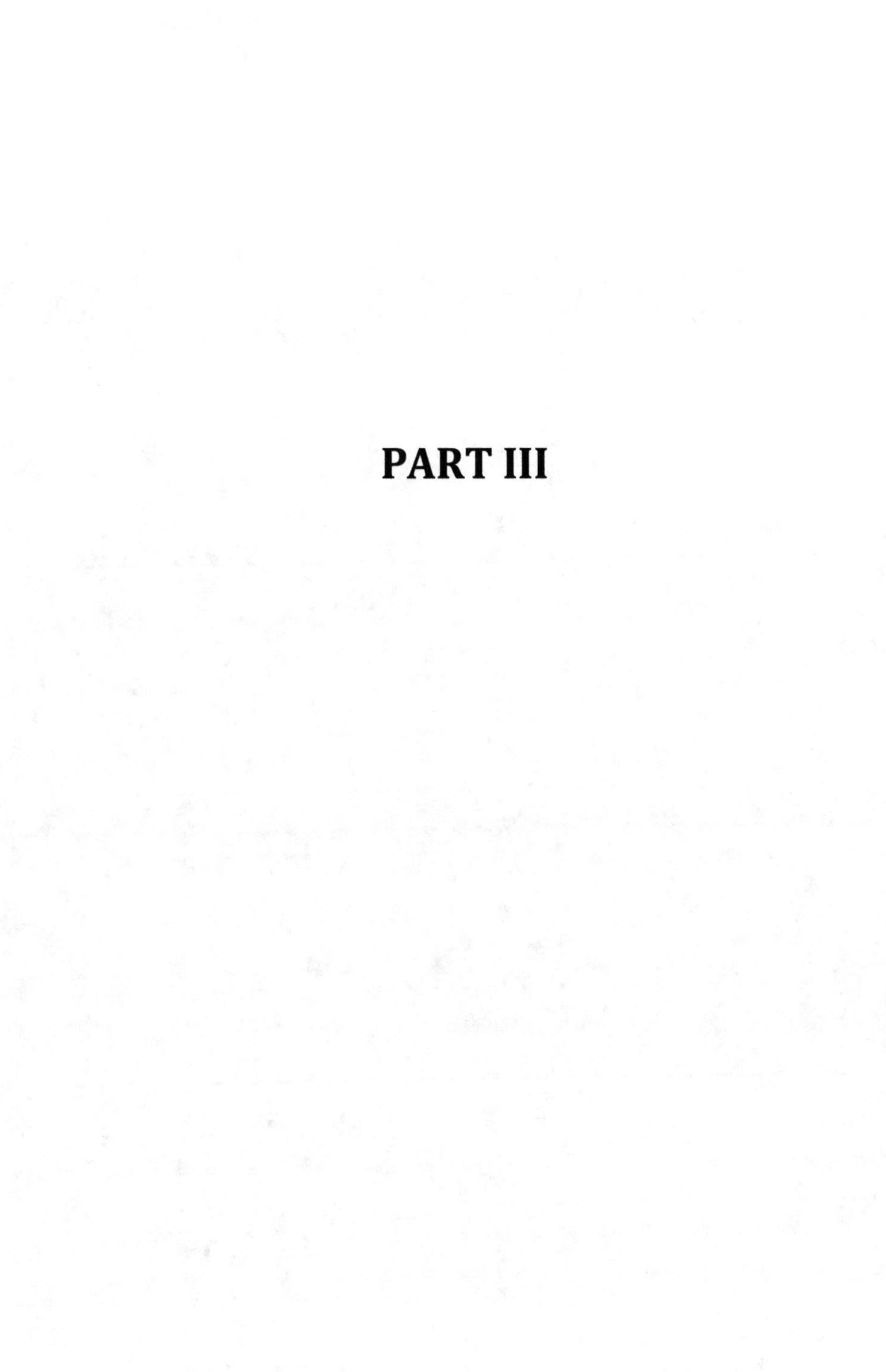

PART III

When he was safely on the other side, Alex turned and watched as the portal behind him disappeared; just as it had done on his last two trips through a door. This time though, Alex looked around and found himself in a beautiful green forest. The tall pines trees grew thick all around him and there was a small creek nearby.

Alex inhaled deeply, taking in the fresh, clean air all around him. "Ah, the aroma of growing pine trees," he said to himself.

He walked to the edge of the water. It was crystal clear and the water shimmered like diamonds as the sun reflected its light on the surface. He looked upstream and found nothing of significance happening in that direction. Then he looked downstream.

Off in the distance, he saw a band of horsemen riding towards him. They were all dressed in clothing much more sophisticated than what he wore in *Jack and the Beanstalk*. Alex needed a change of his outfit, if he was going to blend in with this group of riders. He would have to act quickly, for they were riding hard and approaching fast.

He took out his amulet, and just as he had done before, he used the Talisman of Harmony to change the appearance of his clothing. Instead of the common clothes he had been wearing, he was now dressed in a more stylish looking outfit, made of fine silk, like that of a nobleman.

Alex looked back in the direction of the horsemen. They drew closer and closer. The rider in the lead appeared to be a little distracted, as he was looking to his companion riding along beside him. He was saying something to the friend.

At once, Alex realized the rider did not see him. The rider was almost upon him, and Alex stumbled backwards, falling to the ground. Finally, the horseman saw Alex at the last possible moment and pulled up on his reins, bringing the mighty beast to a halt.

He immediately jumped down from his horse and went straight to Alex to check on him. He bent down on one knee and looked Alex over. Alex noted a look of genuine concern on the man's kind face.

"Are you alright, young man?"

"Yes, sir. I am fine. I guess I just tripped over my feet," laughed Alex, as he got up from the ground.

The man looked him over, once again, to see if there were any scratches, bumps or other injuries.

"I truly am sorry, good sir, I did not see you until the last moment. I guess I was somewhat distracted while talking with my friend over there."

Alex laughed again. "It is Okay. I am just glad you finally did see me."

"Yes," the man agreed. "Otherwise, you might have had a really bad day."

Alex nodded, "Indeed."

Alex looked up at the tall man, as he stood back up. He had a strong physical build and was quite handsome. Unlike his six companions, he was clean-shaven. He had short cropped brown hair and eyes of green both gentle and caring. Like Alex, he too was dressed in fine clothing, but his bore a royal crest on the tunic. His manners were very refined, and he exhibited an air of confidence like that of a Prince.

The man turned and addressed the riders accompanying him.

"Fear not, my friends. The young lad appears to be unhurt. Gentlemen, may I present..."

The man paused for a moment with a puzzling look on his face. He looked back down to Alex.

"I am sorry, good sir, I did not get your name."

Alex bowed before the man and said, "My name is Sir Alex, Your Highness. I am a Knight from a far off kingdom in the North."

"Ah, yes. Good to meet you, Sir Alex. I am Prince Phillip." He smiled, winked at the boy and turned back to the men and said, "I would like to present to you, Sir Alex from the North."

As the prince introduced each of his companions who were still atop their horses, each nodded his head as his name was called out. "Sir Alex, these are my oldest and dearest friends; Erik, Charles, William, Henry, Richard and Thomas."

Alex bowed at the waist before the band of horseman once the introductions were complete.

"It is an honor to meet you all," he said.

One of the men on horseback spoke up and said, "My Prince, we must make our way back to the castle. The time is getting short, and we should begin preparing for the ball."

The Prince turned to the man who spoke, held up his hand, and said, "A moment, please, Erik." Erik sat back on the saddle of his horse and sighed. He was the impatient sort. He had shoulder-length, fiery, red hair and a long scraggly beard to match. He looked more like a Viking rather than a guardsman and friend to the Royal Prince. His blue eyes looked skyward, as he tried to patiently wait for Prince Phillip to finish talking to the young boy.

Phillip turned back to Alex and asked, "So, Sir Alex, what is a young Knight like yourself, doing out here all alone in the forest?"

"I have come here to your kingdom from the Northern territories, representing My Lady, Emagine, to pay her respects to you and your family. She had urgent matters to attend to which did not allow her to make the journey herself, so she sent me in her stead."

Erik could contain his impatience no longer. He pleaded to Phillip, "My Prince..."

The Prince turned back towards his friend and rolled his eyes. "Ah yes, the ball."

"Well, Sir Alex," he said, turning his attention back to the young lad before him, "would you care to join us as we travel back to the castle?"

"Yes, Your Highness, I would."

"Very well then, let us move on."

Erik let out a sigh of relief. Phillip chuckled at his friend's expense. "Someday, Erik, my friend, you will learn to relax."

The other guardsmen laughed. Alex figured it must have been an inside joke.

"Not likely," commented one of the other riders as the laughter continued. Erik frowned and began to sarcastically mock his friends' laughter.

The Prince mounted his horse and reached his hand down and pulled Alex up onto the saddle. He coaxed the horse to move forward, and they started off at a trot. Slowly, the steed sped up to a gallop. Alex began smiling. The smile grew bigger and bigger, the faster they went. He was enjoying the thrill of, once again, being on horseback.

The band of horsemen rode on through the forest and arrived at the castle a short time later.

They rode just inside the castle walls, to where the stables were located. Phillip dismounted his horse, then he reached up to help Alex down from the steed.

"That was an amazing ride, Your Highness. Your skills as a horseman are excellent."

"Thank you, Sir Alex. Riding is one of the things I love most. Sometimes, in my role as Prince, I feel I do not get to ride enough."

"Your Highness, you can just call me Alex, if you would like."

"Very well, Alex, it is." The Prince started to turn, but then he stopped and looked back to Alex. "I am curious, when we first met, how did you know I was a Prince?"

Alex pointed to Phillip and replied, "The royal crest on your tunic was a dead giveaway."

Phillip looked down and smiled.

"You are a very bright young man."

"Thank you, Your Highness."

The two left the stables and went inside the castle. They walked past a number of servile people who bowed before them on their way to the throne room. Phillip was thoughtful enough that he returned each greeting with a nod.

Once in the throne room, the Prince approached his parents, the King and Queen, and bowed his head.

"Father. Mother. I would like to present to you, Sir Alex. He is from the Northern Territories. We met while I was out for my daily ride."

Alex stepped forward and bowed before the King and Queen.

"I am honored to make your acquaintance, Your Majesties."

"It is nice to meet you, Sir Alex. Have you come for the ball?" asked the Queen.

"Yes, indeed I have, Your Majesty. I was sent here on behalf of the Lady Emagine of the North as her representative to pay her respects to both you and to your son, Prince Phillip."

"Thank you, Sir Alex," replied the King. "We hope that tonight's Presentation Ball will give our son, Phillip, the opportunity to meet someone special."

Again, at the mention of the upcoming ball, the Prince rolled his eyes.

"We have invited all of the fair maidens from the kingdom and the surrounding areas to attend. I pray he will find the true love of his life for whom he has sought. Someone with whom he will be happy and will want to spend the rest of his life with as his wife."

"Oh, Sire, I am sure she is out there, and I am sure she will be here tonight."

The Prince turned to Alex and said, "Come Alex. I think we should visit the tailor and see to some clothes you can wear to the ball, tonight."

Alex and Phillip bowed before the King and Queen, then stepped backwards, turned on their heels, and left the throne room. They walked down a hall where the men bowed and the women curtsied to them. At the end of the hall, there was a door that led out to the inner courtyard.

The courtyard was a beautiful and picturesque garden. There was a wide variety of flowers, plants and trees growing all around. The birds were singing and a pair of squirrels were playing together with a walnut on the lush green lawn.

Alex laughed as he pointed out the funny little animals playing what looked like a game of hide the nut.

"Look. The one squirrel grabbed the nut from the other while he wasn't looking, and now he cannot find it."

Phillip laughed as he watched the second squirrel frantically looking around the area for the missing walnut.

"Ah. The wonder and innocence of childhood. Sometimes I wish for the simpler days when I was young. Nothing to worry about. Friends to keep you from being lonely."

"If I may ask, Your Highness, you do not seem to be too excited about the ball tonight. How come?"

"Well Alex, my young friend. Not long ago, my parents tried to arrange a marriage for me. They wanted me to marry a princess from a neighboring kingdom, to strengthen our alliance with her father. I do not know this woman, but from what I had heard of her, we had nothing in common. She too, was against the idea of an arranged marriage. She was in love with another and wanted to be with him. I told my parents that I wanted to marry for love and not for the convenience of the kingdom or for political reasons. For a time, we quarreled over this issue. Finally, a few days ago, my father relented, and he told me that he would host a Presentation Ball. He said he would send out an open invitation to all of the maidens in and around the kingdom. If after the ball, I did not find my one true love, I would have to marry the foreign princess." After a moment, Phillip asked, "What if I do not find her tonight, Alex? Will I be fated to marry someone I do not know or love? Who does not know or love me?"

"Do not worry yourself, Your Highness. I am sure she will be here tonight. The one that will make your heart sing and will forever take away your loneliness and make it a thing of the past."

"I hope that is true, my young friend. In my mind's eye, I can see her there, always calling out to me. But, when life brings my imagination back to reality, she seems far beyond my reach."

"Patience, Your Highness. Have faith that your dreams will soon be realized."

The Prince smiled at Alex. He thought it odd that he found comfort in the assurances from a small child who seemed to think that anything was possible. Phillip started to believe, and with that belief came hope. For the first time, he was actually starting to look forward to the ball that night.

Finally, he looked to Alex and said, "Come, my young friend. Let us go and see to your clothes."

The Prince and Alex left the courtyard behind and walked in the direction of the tailor's shop. When they arrived, Phillip opened the door for Alex, and they went inside.

The tailor and his apprentice began to take Alex's measurements. Phillip pulled the tailor aside and whispered something into his ear. The tailor smiled and nodded agreeably. Once the tailor had the measurements he needed, Alex and the Prince left the shop to allow the workers time to make the clothes.

"Don't they need to measure you, too?"

"They have already made what I will wear tonight at the ball."

"Will they have enough time to finish the clothes I am to wear?"

"My tailor and his apprentice are the fastest in the land. They will have it completed in time. For now, what would you like to do?"

"Oh Your Highness, you do not have to stay with me until the ball. I can always find something to do until then."

"Nonsense. I enjoy your company, Alex. Your words bring me hope and comfort, my young friend. I feel that I can talk to you about anything, even though I just met you a short time ago."

"I have never really had a friend that was a grown-up before. What few friends I do have are much closer to my age."

"Ah, though you are young, you are both kind and wise. Many children your age are more self-centered and think only of their wants and needs. You, on the other hand, are more concerned with the people around you than of your own needs. People like that, both young and old, are hard to find, and they are the most enjoyable persons with whom to keep company. So, what shall we do to pass the time? You really seemed to enjoy the horseback riding. Would you like to go out for a ride?"

"Those horses were huge. What if mine gets scared and takes off?"

"Well, I would imagine we can find a mount more to your size. Come."

Alex and Phillip left the courtyard and headed back towards the stables.

The royal stables were tended by many workers, all bustling, tending to the majestic steeds. The Prince called over to the stable master and talked with him for a moment. Meanwhile, Alex walked about looking at the magnificent mounts. The stable master nodded at the Prince and whistled for one of the stable boys. The stable boy ran to him, bowed to Prince Phillip and listened as the stable master whispered something to him. He nodded that he understood the stable master's instructions and ran off towards the stalls. The Prince thanked the stable master and walked back to where Alex was standing.

He noticed Alex's wide eyed admiration of the beasts and said, "Beautiful creatures, aren't they?"

"Oh yes," replied Alex with a grin from ear to ear.

"It is Okay to pet them. They will not mind."

Alex hesitated a moment.

"Go on. I promise you, it will be Okay."

Alex reached out apprehensively at first, then slowly touched the side of the horse nearest him. When the horse did not object to his touch, he began to rub its side. He looked up to the Prince and smiled.

"He looks very powerful, and yet he seems very gentle," Alex commented.

"Yes. He is one of the gentlest in the whole stable."

The Prince's companions from earlier that day came up to the stables and prepared their horses for riding.

Alex watched them for a moment then turned to Prince Phillip and asked, "Are they your bodyguards?"

"Yes, they are. And, as I mentioned to you earlier, they are also my closest friends. We do many things together. Anytime I leave the confines of the castle, I must take them with me."

The stable boy soon returned to Phillip and Alex, leading a small pony already saddled up.

"What do you think?" asked the Prince, "More your size?"

Alex giggled, looked up to Prince Phillip and said, "Yes. Most definitely."

Then Phillip lifted Alex up on to the pony and placed his feet in the stirrups. He handed Alex the reins.

"There you are, good sir."

"Thank you," replied Alex with a nod and a smile.

The Prince began instructing Alex on how to get the pony to move and how to make him turn.

"To make him go forward, give a slight nudge with your feet along his sides. To stop, pull back on the reins. To turn right, pull slightly to the side with your right hand. And to go left, the opposite? Are you ready to give this a try?"

Alex nodded excitedly, "Yes, I am."

"Very well. Here we go."

The Prince led the pony into the stable's corral area to give Alex a limited and controlled place to learn how to control the animal. After a few laps around the corral and a few turns in either direction, the Prince felt Alex was ready to ride out in the open.

He turned to the stable master who had the Prince's mount saddled up, ready and waiting for him. He went to his horse and mounted up. His companions followed suit, and together, they began riding towards the castle gate.

The group of riders took off from the entrance of the castle and rode out into the forest. For now, they moved along more slowly to allow Alex to become more accustomed to his mount.

"You, my young friend, are a natural horseman," Phillip remarked.

"This is awesome!"

"Awesome?" Phillip looked to Alex with a puzzling expression on his face. "Like big?"

"Where I come from, it is something we say when something is great or thrilling."

"Ah," Phillip smiled. "Well then, yes. This is awesome!"

Alex then prodded his mount to go a little faster. When he was comfortable with that, he sped up a little more. Soon, the pony was riding along at a medium-paced gallop. As they rode on, they passed the stream where Alex and the Prince first met. They continued their ride through the forest and eventually came upon an open field. Then, Alex encouraged his pony to go as fast as it could. Phillip rode close by, ready to spring into action should Alex suddenly need help, but Alex handled the pony rather skillfully.

Alex looked off in the distance and saw that he was heading towards the drop off of a cliff. He pulled back on the reins to slow his mount to a trot. As they got closer to the drop off, he guided the pony up to the edge of the cliff and stopped. The Prince and his companions came up alongside of Alex.

From the ledge, Alex looked down at the land below the cliffs. From this vantage, he saw the mighty palace in all of its glory.

"It is a beautiful home that you have here."

"Yes, it is."

The Prince looked up at the sky. The sun would be setting soon.

"It is now time for us to return to the kingdom. The tailor will soon be finished with your clothes."

"Yes. We would not want to be late for the ball," said Alex smiling at Erik.

"No. We would not!" replied Erik in a serious manner as he leaned forward in his saddle, then he winked at Alex and began laughing. The others joined in the laughter.

The riders settled down and backed their horses away from the ledge, then they turned and began their ride back to the castle. When they arrived, they guided their horses back through the castle gate and into the stables, where they dismounted. The Prince helped Alex down from the pony, and the stable boy took charge of Alex's mount. Alex and the Prince then walked back towards the castle and went inside.

Phillip led Alex to a place where guests usually stayed. The castle guard accompanying them took up station at the door as they went into the room.

Once inside the room, Alex could see that it was adorned with ornate furniture, and there were portrait and landscape paintings hanging on the walls.

"You may use this room to get ready for the ball. The tailor and his apprentice will be along shortly with your clothes. I must go to my room now and get myself prepared, as well. The man standing guard outside will bring you to the ballroom, when it is time."

Alex wrapped his arms around Phillip's waist and hugged him.

"Thank you, and thank you for teaching me how to ride, today. I have never had so much fun as I did today."

Phillip was surprised by Alex's gesture of affection and said, "It gives me great pleasure in knowing that you enjoyed yourself. Someday, when I have a son, I hope he is just as you are." He paused a moment to collect himself, then said, "I shall see you soon at the ball."

The Prince then opened the door. Alex saw him giving instructions to the guard outside, who nodded. Then he left to go down the hallway to his own room. The guard stepped in and bowed towards Alex. "I will be right outside should you need anything." Then he closed the door.

Alex passed the time looking at the art that was hung on the walls in the room. One of the paintings was a portrait of the Prince. He studied the portrait of his new friend. This painting seemed to capture the kind and gentle nature of Prince Phillip, especially his eyes.

Alex continued studying the numerous paintings of the walls of the room for another half hour, or so while he waited.

In time, there was a knock at the door.

"Come in," Alex called out.

The guard opened the door, and Alex saw that the tailor and his apprentice had arrived.

"Sir Alexander, I have your clothes ready for you," said the tailor.

"Wow! You guys really are fast."

The tailor smiled and bowed to Alex.

The apprentice walked across the room and hung the clothes on a wardrobe hook near the chest of drawers. He extended the dressing screen in front of the dresser that would offer Alex some privacy as he changed. Next, he poured some water into a basin that sat on top of the dresser and laid out a washcloth and towel.

"Thank you."

The apprentice bowed his head to Alex, who returned the gesture.

Alex stepped behind the screen and after washing up a bit, he began changing his clothes.

"You and your apprentice did an excellent job," he called out from behind the dressing screen. "I still can't believe you were able to make these clothes as fast as you did and still manage such quality and craftsmanship."

"Thank you for the high praise, Sir," said the tailor. "My apprentice and I pride ourselves on a job well done."

Alex stepped out from behind the screen once he was finished changing to allow the tailor and the apprentice a look at their handiwork. The tailor tilted his head for a moment, then he walked over to Alex and made one final, minor adjustment to the young man's attire. He stepped back to take another look.

"Perfect!" he said finally, as he gestured for Alex to turn around.

Alex turned and looked at himself in the full-length mirror on the wall. He smiled at the image in the mirror before him.

"Yes. It is perfect, indeed."

The tailor and his apprentice tidied up the changing area, gathered up their sewing kits and left the room. As they walked out the door, the guard outside turned and motioned to Alex.

"It is time, Sir Alexander. His Highness, Prince Phillip, is waiting for you to join him."

Alex walked to the open door and stepped out into the hallway. He followed the guard through the hallways, as they walked towards the ballroom.

The inner courtyard of the castle was busy with activity. Horse-drawn carriages were lined up as far back as the outer gatehouse. The carriages rode up to the steps of the palace entrance and dropped off their passengers, who were there to attend the ball.

The arriving guests were led from the inner courtyard to a reception area just outside the ballroom and there, the prominent ones, were presented to the King, Queen and their son, Prince Phillip.

Alex entered the reception area, escorted by the guard. The guard motioned for Alex to continue on and join the Prince. Alex noticed right away that his clothes were an exact match to those that Phillip was wearing, only smaller.

The Prince saw Alex walking towards him and smiled. In turn, Alex smiled back.

Phillip leaned in towards his mother and whispered something to her. The Queen turned her head and looked in Alex's direction. She placed her hand on the King's shoulder, drawing his attention to the approaching young lad. They too smiled at the young man before them. Alex stood tall, as he walked over to Phillip's side.

"Might I say, you look absolutely magnificent," said Phillip.

"As do you, Your Highness."

They both bowed to one another and laughed.

"So. She is here, somewhere?" asked Phillip as he leaned down to whisper into Alex's ear.

"If she is not here now, she will be soon."

"I can hardly wait to meet her. I have waited for this moment for a very long time."

The Queen interrupted when she came to her son's side and asked, "Phillip, shall we all move into the ballroom?"

"Yes Mother, I do believe it is time."

The Royal Family strolled into the ballroom escorted by the young Alex. As they entered the room, the minstrels began to play a royal fanfare from their gallery above that overlooked the ballroom. The Chamberlain tapped his staff three times on the floor as he announced their arrival.

"My Lords and My Ladies, may I present to you Their Majesties, the King, the Queen and their son, His Royal Highness, Prince Phillip. They are accompanied by Sir Alexander, representing the Lady Emagine of the North."

The Royal Family walked past the crowd of people, to the head of the room, and mounted the dais. They turned back towards the gathered masses and the room full of guests bowed before them. The King raised his hands and motioned for everyone's attention.

"I bid welcome to you, one and all. Your King and Queen thank you for your attendance this evening. It is our hope that each of you will enjoy this night of celebration, as we honor our son, Prince Phillip. And without further ado, let the merriment commence."

The guests applauded the King's kind words and on cue from the Queen, the minstrels began to play a waltz. The people began to pair off and dance around the room.

Alex turned to Prince Phillip and coaxed him along. "Well, don't just stand there. Go out among the masses and find her."

The Prince nodded and began making his way around the room where he was introduced, by The Chamberlain, to the many single women in attendance. As he strolled through the crowd, he could hear an argument. He turned towards the disturbance and saw a woman who seemed to be disagreeing with her daughters. The woman and her daughters were very plain and ordinary. The daughters behaved as if they were entitled, like that of two spoiled, little children.

"Both of you act like the ladies you are, and not children," said the woman as she scolded her daughters. "Stop fidgeting, stand up straight, and for God's sake, smile."

The two sisters did as they were told. The woman then turned around and noticed that the Prince was staring directly at them. Her stern demeanor suddenly changed, and she put on a fake smile. She curtsied towards the Prince, while doing so, she muttered under her breath, "The Prince is looking our way. Do not mess up this opportunity for us."

Ignoring protocol, she strolled past The Chamberlain, walked towards the Prince and stopped in front of him. Again she curtsied.

"Your Highness, may I present to you my very lovely and very available daughters."

Phillip was unsure what to do. He wanted to get away from this woman and her daughters, but, at the same time, he did not want to give the appearance of being rude towards the women. So, he put on a happy face and bowed before the threesome.

"So nice to meet you, Madame, and your lovely daughters. It is my hope that you all will have... a... good... time."

Prince Phillip was suddenly distracted by a stunningly beautiful young maiden who just entered the ballroom. He followed her every move, as she strolled about the room. Her elegant, glittering gown was as white as the new snow that sparkled in the morning's sunlight. Her long blonde hair was styled in a way that drew attention to her beautiful, creamy-white face, accented further, by her big, beautiful, blue eyes. All eyes in the room seemed to be fixed on the lovely maiden, except, of course, for those of the woman and her daughters.

Prince Phillip suddenly realized he was being impolite to the lady and her daughters. He snapped his gaze back to the three women before him.

"So nice to have met you," he said as he bowed.

He turned his head once again and looked for the beautiful maiden, then looked back to the mother.

"If you and your daughters would please excuse me, Madame."

The Prince walked back towards the dais. His eyes followed the striking young woman from a distance. He nearly bumped into other guests twice, because he was so distracted. As he walked away from the three women, he could hear the mother chastise her daughters.

"Now see what you have done? Our Prince is walking away. I do not know what I am going to do with you two."

He let out a sigh of relief and smiled, happy to no longer be in the company of that woman and her daughters. It was people like them that gave the aristocracy a bad name. Snobby attitudes and feelings of entitlement were not what he was looking for in a wife, not to mention the outright rude behavior.

When he reached the head of the room, he stepped up onto the dais and just stood there, watching the beautiful maiden from across the room. Alex could see that the Prince was preoccupied with something. He walked over to his side.

"What's wrong?" asked Alex.

Phillip did not respond. It was almost as if he were in a trance. Alex tugged on his sleeve.

"What?" asked the Prince, snapping back to reality. "Oh, nothing is wrong. I think I have just found her, Alex."

Alex followed the Prince's stare. He spotted the beautiful blonde maiden standing across the dance floor. The Prince continued to look at her. There she was, indeed. The most beautiful woman the Prince had ever seen in his life.

Alex nudged the Prince. "What are you waiting for? Go talk to her."

"What do I say to her?"

"Duh! It's a ball, ask her to dance."

"Oh. Right. Ask her to dance. Why did I not think of that?"

"Yes. Why, indeed?" said Alex as he playfully rolled his eyes.

Phillip walked towards the breathtakingly beautiful woman. When he was standing in front of her, he bowed slowly. He noticed that she only wore a single strand of matched pearls, simple yet elegant, unlike some of the other women present who adorned themselves with extravagant jewelry of all shapes and sizes.

"Good evening," he said.

"Good evening, Your Highness."

The maiden curtsied to the Prince and offered her hand to him. Phillip took her hand and gently kissed it.

"I do not think my eyes have ever looked upon such grace and beauty in a woman before now," he said.

The maiden blushed at Phillip's praise. She lowered her eyes for only a moment, then raised them to meet his.

"Would you care to dance?" he asked.

"I would like to very much," she replied with a smile.

Phillip led her to the dance floor. He pulled her close to him, placing his right hand at the small of her back and with his left, taking hold of her tiny hand. He listened for a moment to catch the rhythm of the music, then he stepped into the first of the three beats of the waltz.

Alex walked towards the dance floor to get a better look. He was standing near the older woman and her daughters. The woman appeared to be angry.

"Who is that wretched girl? How dare she take our Prince away from us! What can she possibly have that my own daughters do not?"

"Class?" Alex replied as he snickered. The woman glared down at him. Alex feigned being frightened.

"Why you ungracious little malcontent of a child!" replied the woman, furiously.

He turned and walked away from the three women.

The Prince and the lovely young woman continued dancing. The clock struck nine o'clock, and they still danced, this time to the fast two-step of a rondo. Ten o'clock. Eleven o'clock. They were still dancing. They lost all track of time.

Suddenly, the clock struck twelve, midnight. The beautiful maiden stopped in mid-step, and she looked up at the clock on the wall. "Oh my goodness, the time."

She turned to Phillip and in a rush, she curtsied before him.

"I apologize, Your Highness, but I must go. It is getting late and I must get home, at once."

And, without another word to explain her hasty departure, she turned and ran from the ballroom.

The Prince called out to her, "Wait!"

But she was gone. The Prince stood there for a moment, and Alex walked up beside him.

"You are waiting, again. Go after her," he said as he gave the Prince a nudge.

"Right."

Prince Phillip ran from the ballroom in hot pursuit of the precious maiden.

The young woman ran past the outer reception area, through the hallway, and down a wide staircase leading to the palace door. Once outside, she dashed down the palace steps, to the inner courtyard, where she stopped and frantically searched for her carriage. When she spotted it, she began to run again. She could still hear the clock ringing the twelve chimes of midnight.

As she jumped into the carriage, one of her glass slippers slid off of her foot and landed on the ground. She did not have the time to stop and pick it up. The carriage sped off towards the outer gatehouse and quickly disappeared from sight as it headed for home.

The inner courtyard, where the carriage was parked, grew eerily quiet. There was a sudden flash of black billowy smoke and the dark wizard, Nagama, appeared out of thin air on the palace steps. He walked over to where the glass slipper lay on the ground. He drew his wand and waved it over the slipper. The slipper floated up into his hand.

He studied it for a moment. "Without the glass slipper, the handsome Prince will never find his one true love." Then, without another moment's hesitation, he violently threw it to the ground and laughed. The glass slipper landed on the cobbled ground, shattering into a million pieces. Nagama threw his head back, and cackled louder, then he waved his wand, and he disappeared in another flash of black smoke.

Phillip came running out of the palace entrance a moment later. He looked around anxiously in all directions, trying to catch a glimpse of which way the enchanting young woman went. She was nowhere in sight. Alex came out of the door a moment after that.

"Do you see which way she went, Alex?"

Alex's eyes glanced in all directions around the inner and outer courtyard. Like Phillip, he too saw no sign of the beautiful young maiden, nor did he expect to.

"No, Your Highness. I do not see which way she went."

Alex looked around the inner courtyard for the glass slipper that he knew should be somewhere nearby. Suddenly, he noticed a pile of glass shards scattered on the ground nearby. He walked over to it and bent down to examine the slivers of glass. He shook his head and sighed. Nagama must have paid us a visit, he thought.

Alex stood back up and turned towards Prince Phillip, who was still looking for some sign of which direction the young maiden went. His shoulders sank when he found none. He was saddened at the possibility of never seeing her again. But then determination took over. He raised his shoulders back up, drew in a deep breath, and turned towards his young friend.

"She is the one, Alex. The one I told you about. She is even more beautiful than I could have imagined in my dreams. We must find her."

"Yes I know, and we will find her. I promise you."

"Come, Alex. I must speak to my parents. We must send search parties out to find her."

The Prince turned and walked swiftly back up the steps of the palace. He strolled across the esplanade leading to the door. Alex followed and together, they both went back inside the castle.

Phillip sent word, by way of a palace messenger, for his guardsmen friends to join him in the throne room. As his six companions arrived, they saw the Prince was there talking to his parents, and Alex was at his side. The music and high spirits from the ball continued just down the hallway.

"I cannot understand where she disappeared to so quickly," said Phillip. "I must find her. She is the one I have dreamed of meeting, all of these years. I do not think I could ever be happy without her."

The King asked, "What was her name, Phillip?"

Phillip paused a moment, trying to recall the evening. He shook his head. "Uh, that is another strange thing, Father. I was so captivated by her beauty, I never got around to asking her name."

Alex knew her name, of course, and he wanted to shout it out, but he kept it to himself for the moment. He was pretty sure that it was Nagama who destroyed the glass slipper. He could be anywhere, and Alex had to think of what to do next. He looked on as Prince Phillip and his parents continued to talk.

The Queen finally spoke up. "It is too late to do anything tonight. Tomorrow, my son, you will go out in to the kingdom. You will not stop until you find her."

Phillip smiled at his mother, then he turned around towards his guardsmen. "My friends, I need your help in finding this woman. We will search the kingdom until she is found. Rest up tonight, for tomorrow we ride."

The Prince's friends all snapped to attention at once, and in chorus said, "Yes, Your Highness."

The King smiled at the unconditional loyalty of his son's comrades, and then he turned to Phillip and said, "Your mother and I wish you the best of luck in finding her, my son. Tomorrow, you will go out into the kingdom and find your happiness."

The Prince bowed before his parents, then he wheeled around to Alex, and asked, "Well, my young friend. Would you do me the honor of accompanying me on this quest to find my one true love?"

"Of course, Your Highness. It would be my pleasure."

Alex and the Prince turned and left the company of the King and Queen, who returned to the ball. Phillip led Alex back to the guest quarters so the young lad could rest up for the day to come, then he returned to the ballroom to thank his guests for their attendance and to bid them a good night. When the last of the guests left, Phillip retired to his own room to get some rest.

Alex lay in his bed tossing and turning. He had his mission on his mind. He knew that he was heading for a showdown with the dark wizard Nagama. It was inevitable. He had to be ready when the time came. Then, he remembered the faith and confidence that Lady Emagine had in him and this helped to settle his mind. Soon, he drifted off to sleep.

Hours later, Alex awoke from the nudge of a castle guard. "It is time to wake, Sir Alexander," he said.

Alex got up from his bed and quickly got ready for the day. When he finished dressing, the guard escorted him to where the Prince and his guardsmen had gathered. When Prince Phillip saw that Alex had joined them, he turned to his men and said, "May God's hand guide us in our quest on this day."

"Here, here," the men replied.

Erik playfully shook his head. "Oh, the things we do for love."

Phillip smiled at his friend's humor.

"Fear not, Erik. Someday we may find someone willing to put up with you."

The remaining guardsman chuckled and in chorus, responded, "Not likely."

They all had a laugh at Erik's expense.

"Well, let us get on with it," replied Erik.

"Patient, as ever, my friend," commented one of the other guardsmen.

The band of men did an about face and began marching through the palace hallways, their footsteps echoing throughout the corridors. They emerged from the castle to find the morning sun just beginning to rise.

They went directly towards the stables, where the stable master and stable hands had fresh mounts waiting for them. The pony Alex rode the day before, was saddled up and ready for him to ride. Phillip lifted Alex up onto his mount and then he climbed atop his own steed. He nodded to his companions, and then he prodded his horse to move forward.

"Let us ride, now."

The band of riders rode from the stables and past the outer gatehouse. Once through the castle gate, they headed out into the kingdom.

They traveled from one village to another, searching shops, farms and homes for Phillip's precious maiden. The day wore on. They stopped to ask anyone about the mysterious girl. Most remembered her from the night before, but nobody seemed to know who she was. There was still no sign of her.

After a long day of searching, they came upon a modest looking home. Though it was not as large as some of the other houses in the area belonging to noblemen, it showed immaculate care. The garden and lawns were verdant and green. The trees were pruned and the hedges trimmed.

There was an older woman standing out in front of the home. She was dressed in rather fine clothes, too fine considering the simple home in which she lived. She was watching the Prince, as he and his companions rode up. She waved to Phillip and gestured for him to come forth. The Prince recognized the woman from the night before. It was the mother of the two bickering sisters.

The woman called out over her shoulder to someone in the direction of the house and moments later, her two daughters rushed out of the door. In no time, they were standing beside their mother, straightening their clothes and fussing over their hair.

He hesitated, not wanting to get into another conversation with the woman or her daughters. The last one had been painful enough.

She smiled at the Prince and said with a pasty, phony smile, "Oh, Your Highness. Welcome to my home."

Prince Phillip leaned downed from his horse to address the woman. "Thank you, Madame. I need your help."

"Ah, yes. You have come seeking one of my daughters, haven't you? You wish to have my blessings to court one of them. Right?"

The two daughters smiled and curtsied before the Prince.

The Prince reared back in his saddle and paused a moment, looking for the right words to say.

"Uh. No, Madame. I have been searching throughout this day for the woman with whom I danced all last night. The one who ran from the dance floor at midnight."

"Oh," she said in a cold and disappointed manner. "Her."

"Have you seen her? Do you know where I may find her?"

"No, I do not!" she replied hatefully. Then her demeanor quickly changed back to the phony, pleasant one. "But, why worry about her, when you can take one of my daughters. Either would make you a fine princess. Besides, if that other woman were interested, she would not have run. Right?"

"I apologize for disturbing you, Madame. I must continue my search until I find the girl I seek."

"Well, she is not here."

Prince Phillip sighed. He and his men had searched everywhere he could think of to look. He hung his head in disappointment and coaxed his horse to turn and leave.

"Wait!" cried out a voice from behind.

The Prince pulled back on the reins, stopping the horse, and he turned back towards the voice who had called out. It was Alex who had spoken up.

"She is here," Alex proclaimed. "This woman is her Wicked Step-mother, and those two, there, are her Evil Step-sisters. They are mean and cruel to her. They treat her as a servant and make her clean up after them. Right now, they have her locked up somewhere inside this house."

"How could you know this, Alex?" asked the Prince.

"I just do. Trust me, Your Highness."

The Prince turned his horse to face the woman and her daughters. He leaned forward and glared with anger at them.

"What?" asked the woman. "This ill-mannered little child does not know what he is talking about."

"She lies," replied Alex.

"Well, I have never been as insulted in my life as I am now," said the woman, trying her best to appear like a victim of slander.

Alex guided his pony up next to Phillip, leaned in towards him and softly said, "Your Highness. You know that I am your friend. I would not lie to you. Trust me. She is inside. Have I ever told you anything that was not true?"

The Prince reared back in his saddle again, thought for a moment, and looked to Alex. Then he leaned back in towards Alex, smiled, and whispered back, "No, my young friend, you have not. You told me she would be at the ball last night, and she was."

The Prince then dismounted his horse and gave his full attention back to the older woman.

"Madame, I demand that you allow us entry to search this house or you will suffer the consequences."

"Wait!" she protested, but when she saw the resolve in Phillip's eyes, she resigned and said, "Very well, Your Highness."

Phillip helped Alex down from his pony, and together, they entered the home. They searched room by room, but the young maiden was not there.

"You see," said the woman. "She is not here. This insolent, little child is the one who is lying to you. Not me."

"I am sorry, Alex. She does not appear to be here."

Alex thought for a moment and looked around. He knew that the maiden had to be somewhere in the house. Then he noticed a number of wooden crates stacked up neatly in the nook under the stairwell. He went to the nook and tried to look at what was behind the crates. There, he found a door. He pushed and pulled on the crates, moving them aside.

"Here!" he said excitedly.

He went to the door and tried to open it, but it was locked.

"This door must lead down to the cellar below."

"Madame. The key!" the Prince demanded angrily.

The woman reached into the pocket of her dress and pulled out the key to the door. Slowly, she offered it to the Prince. Her shoulders sank in defeat.

Phillip took the key from her and unlocked the door. The door swung open and revealed a stairwell that led down into the cellar. Both the Prince and Alex hurried down the stairs.

The cellar below was dark and cold. The only light came from up the stairs. They could hear a faint sound of crying. There was someone there in the darkness. Alex found a torch near an old wood burning furnace and lit it. As the light from the torch began to fill the small cellar, Phillip saw a young girl sitting on the floor, crying. She was dressed in tattered clothing. He went to her and knelt down beside her. Reaching out with his hands, he gently lifted her face up to meet his.

"It is you," he pleaded to her.

Even in her ragged clothes, he only saw the woman who so captivated him the night before. His heart exploded with a wide array of emotions: love for the girl before him, concern for what she had been through, hate and contempt for the Step-mother and her daughters.

The girl looked into the Phillip's eyes and said, "You came for me."

He helped her up off of the floor and gently guided her onto a nearby boxed crate.

She reached down and from behind her tattered apron, she pulled out a glass slipper.

He took the glass slipper from her tiny hands and placed it on her foot. It fit her like a glove. His heart swelled at the realization of finally finding the other half of his heart, and he smiled at her. He took her into his arms; they embraced.

He whispered softly into her ear, "I don't even know your name, and yet, I want to spend the rest of my life with you."

She pulled back just far enough to look into his eyes, caressing his face with her gentle hands and said, "Cinderella. My name is Cinderella."

"I am Phillip."

She smiled and replied, "Yes, I know."

Then, he kissed her. It was a long and passionate kiss.

Alex covered his eyes and giggled.

When their lips parted, Phillip turned his head and looked back over his shoulder at the Step-mother and her daughters. His eyes reflected the rising anger that began to fill his soul at the mere sight of these women.

"Arrest them!" he commanded to his guardsmen.

He turned his attention back to Cinderella, and suddenly, the anger inside him washed away, and serenity returned to his face. Joyfulness filled his heart and his eyes began to mist over as he looked into her heavenly blue eyes.

"I know that we have only begun to know one another, but I have been waiting for you to come into my life for a very long time. Would you do me the honor of becoming my wife?"

"Yes," she replied, "I can think of nothing I want more than to be your wife."

Phillip kissed Cinderella, again.

Cinderella then surprised the Prince with the next words she spoke. "I know that you are angry with how my family has treated me, but for a wedding present, I ask that you not arrest them. They may have not treated me with kindness, but I do not wish them to be put in prison. I wish to show them the mercy, they never showed me. It is my wish that they be stripped of all they own and cherish, and then they be banished from the kingdom for the remainder of their lives."

He considered her words carefully for a long moment, trying hard to understand how she could be so compassionate, seeing the life she had led at the hands of her family. "You are a very forgiving person considering what they have done to you." Then, after another long moment, he nodded and said, "It will be done as you wish, my dearest Cinderella."

He turned back to his men and commanded, "Make it so."

He stood up and helped Cinderella up from where she sat on the crate and began walking her towards the stairs leading up from the cellar. They stopped in front of the woman and her daughters.

"Madame, and I use that term loosely," he said. "You and your daughters are to be stripped of all title and privilege, and you are hereby banished from this kingdom." He leaned in towards the woman and in a low, firm voice said, "If you should ever show yourselves here while my family rules, you will be arrested at once, and put into prison for the remainder of your lives. Is there anything about what I just said that you do not understand?"

The Step-mother hung her head. "No, Your Highness, I fully understand the terms of our release."

"Remove them from my sight," commanded Phillip.

The Step-mother and her daughters turned to leave the house to begin their new lives in exile escorted by the Prince's men.

Phillip took Cinderella by the hand and led her up the stairs from the cellar.

He guided her towards the front door of the house, but she hesitated at the threshold. Phillip stopped and turned to Cinderella. He tried to reassure her, "It is alright. No one will ever do you harm, again."

"It is not that, my love," she replied. She looked down at the tattered clothing she wore. "Before I leave my old life behind and begin my new life with you, I would like to freshen up a bit. These are not the clothes to wear when meeting the King and Queen for the first time."

"Very well, my darling. My men will see to the horses outside. Alex and I will wait for you here."

Cinderella excused herself and she went upstairs to change. The Prince and Alex waited by the fireplace. The guardsmen waited outside, tending to the horses, getting them ready for the journey back to the palace.

The Prince looked to be in a daze. Alex went to his side.

"Are you alright, Your Highness?"

"What?" he snapped out of his daydream. "Oh, I am sorry, Alex. I guess I am a little numb, realizing that my dream has finally come true. Even dressed in the rags she wore, Cinderella, is by far the most beautiful woman I have ever met, and unlike some women, her beauty is not only on the outside, but it is within, as well."

"She is indeed a lovely person," Alex agreed.

Their conversation was interrupted a short time later, when they heard footsteps coming back down the stairs. Cinderella wore a modest dress.

"I am sorry, my Love. This is the best dress that I have. My Step-mother allowed me to have only one nice dress. It was more for show when others were around."

"You look absolutely beautiful. Wouldn't you agree, Alex?"

"Yes, I would, Your Highness."

"Is there anything here, in which you would like to take with you?" asked the Prince.

Cinderella looked around the house for a moment, then turned back to the Prince and replied, "No. I only have bad memories of this place. There is nothing from this life I wish to take into the next."

"What then should we do with the house and the possessions within it?"

"I would like for the house and everything in it to be sold at a fair price. The money raised by the sale should be given to help the sick and the poor. It seems only right that this place, which holds so many unhappy memories for me, should be put to use to make life for others less of a burden."

Phillip smiled at her sincere desire to help others.

Together, they walked outside, where his men waited. He gently lifted Cinderella up onto his horse, placing her in the saddle with her legs dangling to one side. Then he mounted up as well, sitting just behind her. They prepared themselves to leave for the castle, to begin their new lives together.

Suddenly, the late afternoon skies grew dark as black ominous clouds rolled in. A bolt of lightning shot down from the heavens above and struck the ground, nearly missing the Prince and Cinderella. The ground beneath them shook as it erupted in fire and smoke. The abrupt and loud blast startled Phillip's horse, and it bucked upward like a crazed and untamed beast.

Knowing that he could not stay mounted on the frightened steed, Phillip instinctively wrapped his arms around his beloved Cinderella. His horse continued to buck and twist, and finally the Prince lost his grip on the reins, throwing the couple to the ground below. When they hit the earth, Phillip tucked and rolled, taking the brunt of the impact unto himself.

He looked into Cinderella's frightened eyes and asked, "Are you hurt?"

After a long moment, a dazed Cinderella mustered the strength to reply. "No, I am unhurt, my love."

Phillip rolled up and away from her until he was up on one knee. His hand reached down for the grip on his sword, ready to draw it and defend Cinderella at all costs.

As the flames dissipated and the smoke cleared, a black-cloaked figure stood there before them. The evil wizard, Nagama, had returned, and he was angry. He glared at Alex.

"You shall not win this time; whoever you are. I shall destroy you! Them! And then, I shall lay waste to this land! There will be no happy ending for the Prince and Cinderella if I have anything to say about it."

The Prince's guardsmen sprang into action. Each man drew his sword and charged towards Nagama, in a futile attempt to protect their Prince. Nagama aimed his wand towards them and a bolt of fire shot from its tip, striking the ground in front of the Prince's protectors. The terrain before them exploded with an incredible blast, and the shockwave knocked the soldiers from their feet. Most of the men were too stunned by the explosion to act, the rest fell to the ground unconscious.

Alex moved in closer to the Prince and Cinderella. Phillip began to draw his sword, but Alex covered the Prince's hand in an effort to stop him from pulling his blade.

"No, Your Highness," he cried out. "I cannot permit you to risk your life."

Alex reached inside his tunic and pulled something out. It was the Talisman of Harmony. He prepared for the battle to come.

He turned to face the dark wizard, Nagama.

"My name is Alex DaSilva, and I am here to see that you do not have anything to say about it."

Nagama was stunned by the brash authority of the little boy standing before him. He cackled an evil laugh. As Phillip rose to his feet, he pulled his sword from its sheath and yelled.

"Alex! Run!"

"No, Your Highness. This is why I was brought here. Only I have the means and the power to stop him."

"A boy? To stop me? What was the Council thinking? Did they think a mere child can stop me? Do they not realize the power that I possess? When I am finished here, and you are slain, I will move on to the next tale and destroy any chance of a happy ending there, too. And, when I have taken all the happiness from those places, I will lay siege to the Council, itself. I will enslave the Council members, and they will be forced to do my bidding."

"You seem pretty sure of yourself," taunted Alex.

"You shall see."

Nagama raised his wand again and pointed it towards Cinderella and the Prince. He began speaking in a foreign tongue, reciting a killing spell.

"*Animo uri et in hora mortis invoco!*"

A white, hot flame shot out from the wand and streaked towards the young lovers. With no time to think, Alex stepped in front of them with the Talisman at the ready. He began speaking the magical words of the spell Lady Emagine had taught him.

"*Amor, et pacem!*"

The white, hot flame was drawn into the Talisman, where its power was absorbed. The power within the Talisman began to surge and build up. The intensity became greater and greater with each passing second. Finally, it was so powerful that Alex found it difficult to maintain his hold on to the Talisman. Just as he felt his grip start to slip, the amulet shot out a ray of blinding bright light that raced towards the evil wizard. The light surrounded and enveloped him. At first, Nagama struggled. Then, when he realized there was nothing he could do, that he was powerless to stop the enchanted light, he cried out.

"No! You will not defeat me. No!"

The pure light consumed every essence of Nagama, and he faded away, as if he were enveloped by a fog. With Nagama trapped, the ray of light was reabsorbed into the Talisman, imprisoning Nagama there inside.

The dark clouds rolled away, and once again, it was a calm and beautiful sun-lit afternoon.

Phillip raced to Alex's side to ensure that he was alright.

"Are you hurt, my friend?"

"No, Your Highness. I am fine. This Talisman protected me from Nagama's evil spell."

"Thank God! And, thank you. You have saved all of our lives, some of us, in more ways than one."

Phillip then turned his attention to his men. "I must see to my friends." He and Alex went to each of the guardsmen, to check on them. They were still stunned by the explosion, but each would recover.

When the Prince was sure his men's immediate needs had been met, he joined Alex, who was now standing with Cinderella. Alex assured the Prince that she was unhurt. Phillip smiled at the brave, young lad before him.

"I have a request of you, Alex. I wish that you would stand with me as my witness, when I take Cinderella to be my wife."

Alex paused a moment. He looked around to see if the door leading back to the hallway had reappeared. It had not. He turned back to Phillip and smiled.

"It would be my honor to stand with you, Your Highness."

"Come then, my friend. We have a wedding for which to plan and prepare."

The guardsmen had rounded up the horses which had scattered during the confrontation.

Phillip lifted Alex up onto his pony. He then turned back to Cinderella, gently lifting her back up onto his horse, and then he himself mounted the steed. The company of riders departed the village, riding back towards the castle.

The following day, the bells from high atop the cathedral and in the churches throughout the kingdom could be heard tolling. The people were in the streets all over the kingdom, celebrating the marriage of Prince Phillip to Cinderella.

The King and Queen sat on their thrones near the altar, while Phillip and Cinderella stood before them. Alex was at their side. The Bishop, from the church where the Royal Family attended Sunday services, performed the wedding ceremony.

Phillip and Cinderella chose to write their own vows and share the feelings they felt for one another with the congregation of people before them.

After they exchanged vows, the Bishop said, "You have both given your declarations of love to one another. And, now, by the power granted to me by God, I pronounce you husband and wife." The Bishop turned to the Prince and smiled. "You may now kiss your bride."

Phillip lifted Cinderella's white veil and gently caressed her face. He pulled her to him and kissed her on the lips. The cathedral erupted with the sound of cheers and applause. The jubilation soon spread to the streets outside. The Prince and his new Princess, turned towards the masses. The people bowed, and in return, the Royal couple bowed.

Suddenly there was a shimmering light and the doorway magically reappeared. Phillip looked to Alex. Alex offered a reassuring smile to his friend.

"It's Okay. I must go now, Your Highness. That magical door will take me back to where I come from."

"I understand, my dear, young friend. We both thank you for all you have done for us and know that we shall never forget you. When the time comes, we will name our first child in your honor."

Alex bowed before Prince Phillip and the Princess Cinderella.

"I am happy to have been of service to both you, and your lovely bride."

Phillip knelt and wrapped his arms tightly around Alex.

He whispered in his ear, "Thank you for helping me find her."

"You are most welcome."

Cinderella came to Alex. She too bent down and hugged him. She kissed him on the cheek.

"I fear that my life would have turned out much differently than it is now, had you not come here. Thank you, from the bottom of my heart."

"I am so happy for you both."

Phillip and Cinderella stood back up and watched as Alex walked to the door. Alex turned back to them and smiled. They smiled in return. Alex waved to them, turned and went through the door.

The bright light once again appeared and disappeared.

Lady Emagine was there waiting for his return. She was smiling.

"You have done it, Alex. You have saved us all. The words, 'Thank you,' just do not seem to be enough to show my gratitude for what you have done."

"What about *Beauty and the Beast*?"

"See for yourself."

Lady Emagine walked to the door that led to *Beauty and the Beast*. She reached out, turned the doorknob and the door opened. Alex smiled.

"You see? Just as I told you. All the evil that Nagama has done has now been undone. What was before is now, again. We owe you everything."

"I am glad that I was able to help."

"And now it is time for you to return to where you came from. On behalf of the Council of Tales, I thank you."

Alex looked to Lady Emagine and smiled. He reached up for the chain around his neck that held the Talisman of Harmony. He removed the Talisman and gazed at it a moment. It was still hard to believe that this charm he held in his hands saved his life and that of the lives of Prince Phillip and Princess Cinderella. He offered it back to Lady Emagine.

"Here, I should return this before I go."

Lady Emagine held up her hand and said, "No. The Talisman is yours, now. The only safe place for it, if there is one, is with you in your world. The essence of Nagama is trapped inside the Talisman.

His followers would stop at nothing to free him from the prison in which he now resides."

"Will I ever see you again?" he asked.

"Every time you read a story, I am there with you in spirit, Alex. As to whether or not we will ever come face to face again, I cannot answer."

"Well, if you ever need me again, know that I am forever at your service."

"Of this, I never had a doubt. You will be forever remembered by those of us who safeguard the tales of mankind. I bid you farewell and safe journeys."

Alex bowed and said, "Goodbye, Lady Emagine."

Lady Emagine reached out and gently touched Alex on his shoulder.

Suddenly, Sarah was waking Alex up.

"Wake up, sleepy head."

Alex opened his eyes and looked around. He was back in his own room. He sat up in his bed and rubbed his eyes.

"Was it all a dream?"

"Was what all a dream, honey?"

"Well last night after you read me my story, I fell asleep. I woke back up, and I was in this hall that had a thousand doors. I couldn't find you, so I thought maybe you were inside one of the rooms behind the doors. I opened one of them, went inside, and suddenly, I was in the story of *Rumpelstiltskin*."

Sarah took a seat on the side of Alex's bed, and listened as he continued his story. He told her all about his exciting journey into *The Hall of a Thousand Doors.*

"And then Lady Emagine thanked me for saving them, and she touched my shoulder. That was when you woke me up."

"Oh my. Sounds like you had a wondrous adventure."

"Yeah," he said disappointedly. "But now, I know it was only a dream."

"Well, dreams are what make us special. Without our dreams, we wouldn't have anything to look forward to and life would be pretty boring."

"I guess so."

"Okay. Time to get a move on. You are running behind and you are going to be late for school. Hurry up and get ready. I will go and make your breakfast. Oh, and don't forget to make your bed."

"Yes, Ma'am."

Sarah smiled at her son. She got up and left the room.

Alex climbed off of the bed and began to straighten the covers. He heard something fall off the other side of the bed. Curious as to what it was, he walked around to the other side.

There, on the floor, was a chain sticking out from under his bed. Whatever it was attached to, had gone under the bed. He knelt down, reached for the chain and pulled on it. He raised the chain up to his eyes. Attached to the other end of the chain was the Talisman of Harmony. His eyes grew wide. He stood and went over to his bookshelf. He ran his finger across the titles. He stopped at *Beauty and the Beast* and pulled it out. Alex opened the book and turned it to the end. He silently read the last few lines of the story. Then he read the last line aloud.

"And they lived happily ever after."

Alex looked up from his book.

"Mom!"

EPILOGUE

Black clouds swelled about the sky in a far off, unknown place. The land was barren of any plant life, save a dead tree here and there. In the distance, there was a dark and foreboding castle. Its shadowy colored stones barely gave notice to the flashes of lightning that were dancing all across the gloomy skies.

A rider approached the ominous castle, riding hard and fast. His black cloak buffeted in the wind as he rode on. The rider pulled up as he entered the castle's gate. He dismounted his beast and quickly made his way into the castle.

His footsteps through the hallways were marked by the sound of his heavy boots striking the floor, echoing throughout the castle. The passageways were dimly lit by torches along the walls.

He walked into the castle's great hall where his comrades had gathered. One sat on a makeshift throne, while the other nine stood before him. The rider stopped before the man sitting on that throne, and he took a knee.

"My Lord Morthane. I bring grave news," he said.

He waited to be acknowledged before continuing.

"Speak your grave news, Krell."

"Your father, my Lord Nagama, has been defeated."

Morthane stood up in outrage. "What! How can this be? My father is a great and powerful wizard."

Krell continued his report.

"The Council of Tales brought in an outsider to stop him. I cannot find out where he is being held, only that he has been imprisoned. The Council's champion has disappeared, as well. There were reports that this champion was nothing more than a mere child."

"A mere child? It would take more than a mere child to defeat my father."

Morthane paused a moment, and then said, "My friends, make yourselves ready. We will pay the Council a visit this day and force them to release Lord Nagama to us. Should they refuse, we will gather our armies and lay siege to the Council and destroy it once and for all."

Morthane marched forward to leave the Great Hall. He and his men filed down the darkened hallways of the black castle to the stables outside. Each man, dressed in a black cloak, mounted his horse and prepared to ride. They all turned to Morthane, waiting for him to give the word.

Morthane slapped the hindquarter of his horse. The beast bucked upwards and reared back in a loud protest.

He looked out towards the North and yelled, "Let it begin!"

The steed leapt forward and sprinted off towards the outer gate. Morthane's men followed closely behind him. Their cloaks thrashed in the wind like a moving wave of black.

About The Author

Christopher Sturdevant was born on the island of Taiwan in 1965, while his Father served in the United States Air Force. In 1971, the family moved to San Antonio, Texas, where he grew up.

He began writing poetry and short stories in high school. Years later, when he began to learn to play guitar, he added songwriting to his list of writing talents.

Upon graduation from high school, he followed in his Father's footsteps and entered the military, where he trained as a medic. Since then, he has worked in the fields of mental health, computer sales, technical support, digital media, web design, and the copy and print industry.

In 2012, he graduated *Suma Cum Laude* from Northwest Vista College, in San Antonio, Texas, with a Digital Media degree.

Today, Chris spends much of his free time working on the sequel to this novel, and he is well on his way to completing another exciting adventure featuring child-hero, Alex DaSilva. The story of Alex's journey in *The Hall of a Thousand Doors* will unfold over a series of several books, however, Chris is already in the planning stages of several stand-alone novels based on the original characters from this series.